HALF-LIVES

HALF-LIVES

STORIES

LYNN SCHMEIDLER

AUTUMN
HOUSE PRESS
Pittsburgh, PA

DESIGN: Kinsley Stocum | AUTHOR PHOTO: Alison Sheehy
COVER ART: *Design for Textile* (ca. 1808–10), Anonymous

Grateful acknowledgment is made to the editors of the following publications, in which these stories first appeared: "Sex Was Everywhere," *Hobart* (as "In the 70s, Everyone, Including Mannequins, Had Nipples") | "The Wanting Beach," *Conjunctions* | "Corpse Pose," *Kenyon Review Online* | "The Future Was Vagina Forward," *Hunger Mountain Review* | "The Audio Guide," *The Southern Review* | "InventEd," *BOMB*, Winner of the 2023 Fiction Contest | "Being Stevie," *The Georgia Review*, and a *Best American Short Stories 2015* Notable | "Half-Lives," *The Georgia Review* | "Plural Like the Universe," *The Southern Review* | "Happy Birthday," *Hags on Fire* | "The Time Museum," *No Tokens*

LIBRARY OF CONGRESS CATALOGING-IN-PUBLICATION DATA
NAMES: Schmeidler, Lynn, 1967- author.
TITLE: Half-lives : stories / Lynn Schmeidler.
OTHER TITLES: Half-lives (Compilation)
DESCRIPTION: Pittsburgh, PA : Autumn House Press, 2023.
IDENTIFIERS: LCCN 2023048251 (print) | LCCN 2023048252 (ebook) | ISBN 9781637680919 (paperback ; acid-free paper) | ISBN 9781637680926 (epub)
SUBJECTS: BISAC: FICTION / Short Stories (single author) | FICTION / Absurdist | LCGFT: Short stories.
CLASSIFICATION: LCC PS3619.C44525 H35 2023 (print) | LCC PS3619.C44525 (ebook) | DDC 813/.6--dc23/eng/20231027
LC record available at https://lccn.loc.gov/2023048251
LC ebook record available at https://lccn.loc.gov/2023048252

Autumn House Press is a nonprofit corporation whose mission is the publication and promotion of poetry and other fine literature. The press gratefully acknowledges support from individual donors, public and private foundations, and government agencies. This book was supported, in part, by the Greater Pittsburgh Arts Council and the Pennsylvania Council on the Arts, a state agency funded by the Commonwealth of Pennsylvania.

pennsylvania
COUNCIL ON THE ARTS

GREATER PITTSBURGH
ARTS COUNCIL

Arts loud and clear

TABLE OF CONTENTS

HALF-LIVES

SEX WAS EVERYWHERE

ONCE UPON A TIME there was no sex, but sex was every-where: in Lisa's sixth-grade locker with her breath mints and roll-on deodorant; in Dr. Perlman's walk—slow and tight-calved; in Mr. Robinson's guitar, playing Cat Stevens' "Wild World" each afternoon before the bell; in Mrs. Tay-lor's wavy, knee-length red hair, smelling of Wella Balsam and cigarettes. Sex was in the heat that gathered under the ceiling of the gym—when you climbed the rope to the very top, you came down smelling of it. Sex was baked into the raviolis Gina's mom pinched shut around spoon-fuls of meat while Gina snuck thick slices of last night's chocolate cake for you to share upstairs as you admired her confirmation dress, all white eyelet and pearls. Sex was in John O'Connor's towheaded curls, limp on his damp scalp as he leaned in to marvel at the hugeness of your thighs.

There were strong urges in contradictory directions: Gina's older half brothers, so shaggy and sideburned that you asked to take your plate up to Gina's room so you wouldn't have to face them over dinner. Then you spied on them from the top of the stairs, blood pounding in your throat with every swallow. And Sam in your class, who you wanted to press against the wall and kiss, and whom you kicked instead, so hard he turned on you and screamed "what's wrong with you?"

See Eros (life force) and Thanatos (death drive) in later psychoanalytic theory.

It was a land where everything was safe until it wasn't: Ted Bundy, arm in a sling, waiting for you by every car. It was a land where you walked two blocks from school to the Luncheonette for a dollar twenty-five hot dog special, followed by a school-wide assembly introducing the Safe House program—"look for the orange SAFE HOUSE card in the front window if you need to ring the bell," too late for little Maria-of-the-transparent-skin who'd returned to school with bruised cheeks and bloody veins in the whites of her eyes. And Mr. McMann was suddenly no longer the boys' swim team coach because he was a "bachelor." And Maggie told her mother something that made her mother fire the babysitter and then every week Maggie talked to a doctor named Leda while her mother waited in the car outside.

Once upon a time there was no sex, but sex was everywhere, and there were body parts. Gina leaned into the window of a lost driver's car to answer his question and his purple penis was propped against the steering wheel. Lisa's father slept naked, and when you slept over, you saw his long white buttocks as he left the bathroom in the middle of the night (like quivering poached pears). One day, Teo, a distant older cousin from Israel, appeared and told your little brother (who told you) he liked to lick salt off girls' breasts. The gardener's son, rumored to be a rapist, worked shirtless in the backyard doing things to the flowers; his back rolled and glistened like a buttered croissant.

There was food. There was a seven-ounce smoked gouda devoured during *General Hospital*, followed by graham cracker sandwiches filled with Betty Crocker cream cheese frosting during *Edge of Night*. There were stomachaches, and there were fantasies of Baryshnikov and David Cassidy.

Insert here a feminist history of gorging and female sexual repression from the primordial to the postmodern.

Once upon a time there was no sex, but sex was everywhere, and there was fever. It was the year of the chicken
pox and then the extended family cruise on the *Staten-
dam*: Mothers in halter tops and Bermuda shorts sitting
outside in the sun, silver reflectors under their chins, when
you fell asleep on your stomach by the pool and your back
crisped so that nothing—not Noxzema, not vinegar, not
leaning forward for a week—nothing brought relief and
you glowed heat and untouchability. And your sister sleep-
walked onto the ship's deck (she could have walked right
off the boat into the moony ocean), and then went back to
the bunk across from yours and snored with her mouth
wide open beneath the ledge with the pennies she must
have swallowed since they were gone the next morning.
The rest of the week, your cousins calling, "Hey Drea, got
change for a nickel?"

Once upon a time there was no sex, but sex was everywhere, and there were words whose meanings you pretended to know—ménage à trois and fellatio. And there
were jokes whose punch lines you pretended to understand—Why does Dr. Pepper come in a bottle? Because
his wife died. It was a land of intimations. There were
Annie and Esme who cleaned the house on Tuesdays and
Thursdays (lived together, had no boyfriends). There was
the piano tuner who was a man one time and a woman the
next (Philip to Philippa). There was *Harold and Maude*.

Once upon a time there was no sex, but sex was everywhere, and there were rumors: Mrs. Donoghue (divorced) and Mr. O'Hara (single) team-teaching, winking over your head. There was Lisa at the end-of-school dance, arms around Timmy's neck. Why had you never seen him before tonight? And how had he gotten so tall without your noticing? There was the rock star whose stomach was pumped because of all the semen he'd swallowed, and Peter's sister's best friend who got pregnant from a toilet seat after *her* best friend got pregnant from her boyfriend's pee. There were live gerbils and dill pickles in all the wrong places, and there was the spider that laid eggs in some girl's cheek so when she scratched what she thought was a mosquito bite, hundreds of baby spiders crawled out of her face.

Banisters were for straddling. The stuffed unicorn was for rubbing between your legs and then throwing in the trash when its horn smelled.

Once upon a time there was no sex, but sex was everywhere, and there was fear. There was the drainage hole in the stone wall that opened into nothing but air over the quicksand inlet at the end of the dead-end block. And there was your neighbor Jimmy—square-chinned, squint-eyed, and broody—who you dreamed of kissing before he tripped on his stairs with his fishing rod in hand and the end of the rod went through his eye and into his brain. You stayed up all night praying he would live, that if God let

him live, you'd be kinder to your siblings and less fresh to
your parents, and he did live, but he was never the same. It
wasn't just the cane and the stiff leg.he had to grab by the
thigh and swing around the side when he walked. His face
was crooked and he was moved to the special ed class,
and when your parents invited his family over for dinner
and your father asked him what piece of chicken he pre-
ferred ("I'm a leg man because the leg never gets old, are
you a breast man, Jimmy? Come on, you're a breast man,
right?") he just sat there with a half-grin on his face, and
you wondered if your prayers for him to live were not specific enough.

Once upon a time there was no sex, but sex was everywhere, and there was competition. There was Steven on
his bike on your way home from school who you were supposed to ask to the square dance on Gina's behalf, but who
you managed to get to ask you first. There were tie-dyed
shirts cut into strips at the bottom onto which you threaded
wooden beads that clacked and clapped as you walked so
Timmy would turn away from Lisa when you entered the
room. There were dances you danced at the talent show
so the boys could see your hips and poems you wrote for
class so the boys could hear your voice. There were boys
too skinny and boys too dull, boys not smart enough and
boys not mean enough. Boys whose chairs you pulled out
when they were about to sit down and boys you made sure
you were cast opposite in plays.

Once upon a time there was no sex, but sex was everywhere, and there were placebos—hooker costumes on Halloween, sleeping bags in the wayback of the station wagon. Catwoman and hot pants. Chest hair peeking out of collars and wrap skirts that flew open in the wind.

Once upon a time there was no sex, but sex was everywhere, and there was a whole rich life of love. There were afternoons on the front lawn loving back walkovers and back handsprings, and there was running barefoot to meet the Good Humor truck at the end of the street (pretending the ice cream was for your little sister) and cutting your foot on a piece of glass and Lucy from up the street with her choker made of hemp, smelling like bubble gum and sixteen-year-old-girl sweat, lovingly carrying you back home. It was a land of tube tops and velour and somewhere in the future were your very own children waiting to be slung over your shoulder like the most adorable purse straps. There were swans' nests in the reeds across the inlet at the end of the block. Potato bugs and daddy longlegs. Black-eyed Susans at the garden wall and, after two weeks in Vermont, a gigantic sunflower—dad-tall, plate wide—nodding its weird love.

Not everybody's father was as handsome as yours. Lisa and Gina liked to come over and watch him play the guitar, admiring how his hands moved up and down the fretboard.

This section left intentionally blank.

Once upon a time there was no sex, but sex was everywhere, and there were dreams—hiding that you could fly until you couldn't take it anymore, then flapping your arms hard and taking off over roofs, naked and slick; dropped overboard from a boat and sinking to the bottom before realizing if you sucked hard, you could breathe underwater, slowly, thickly.

You were movie stars and murderers in the making. Some of you had big plans. Others went along. Two of you designed a restaurant that served only breakfast and dessert. Afterward, you made and sold painted dough pins in the shape of meaningful and repeatable objects— hearts, moons, roller skates. You were entrepreneurs and chauvinists and other French-sounding things.

Once upon a time there was no sex, but sex was everywhere—and there was death. There was the boy on his bike on his way to school caught under the eighteen-wheeler who you offered a minute of silence to during first period, though the principal wouldn't say his name over the loudspeaker, and you couldn't picture how it had happened and you couldn't stop picturing how you almost could picture the truck on your bike, on your leg, on your chest. There was the Billig boy diving into the shallow end of the pool. There was the girl who walked onto the neighbor's frozen pool and fell in and couldn't get out and no one heard her or held her or saw her as she died, blue and alone. There was *Jonathan Livingston Seagull* all summer long, on the boat in swells—you were limitless, your body your own idea—with your parents saying, "when are you going to get your head out of your book and live a little?"

THE WANTING BEACH

OUR MOTHER—GULL TATTOOED across her chest, wish-bones for hairpins—told us never to go to the Wanting Beach. She had. We thought this explained her eyes: They looked at you and you contracted, something inside you was sucked out, gone. No one looked our mother in the eye more than once.

But we were girls, models of curiosity. All three of us. We didn't listen. We each wanted a particular boy, so we went to the Wanting Beach with a thread from his sleeve, a wad of gum he'd spat on the road, a pebble he'd kicked. We were tracing the boys' initials in the sand with our big toes when three shadows fell over our feet, and we turned to see their shoulders at our lips.

"What's this?" said the boys' voices in our hair. They were hovering over us, watching our feet in the sand.

We were embarrassed and so continued to write as if we had not been writing their initials, but were instead spelling different secret wishes, but every next letter pulled us deeper into our want. Then they bent and each put a hand over one of our feet and looked up at us and we saw our mistake: The Wanting Beach was not where you went to get what you wanted—it was the beach that wanted. The beach wanted and wanted and filled us with its want until we were nothing but bottomless want-buckets, impossible to fill.

We wanted these boys and these boys wanted us, but you cannot want and also have. The boys realized their mistake, too. Their eyes kept taking bits of us, and our eyes kept taking bits of them. And so, we stayed like that, looking into each other's eyes, taking as much as we lost until we were empty of we and they were empty of they. And when they were full of we and we were full of they, the tide turned and the wanting reversed—we wanting we back from them and they wanting they back from us. On the Wanting Beach everything was always shifting, aching, piling wrack lines of nets and bones and broken sparkling things.

Getting to the Wanting Beach had been easy, like finding dimes in a vending machine. Leaving was harder. We could not find our shoes in the moonless night, and we lost our sense of direction. We wandered, first holding hands with the boys, then holding hands with each other, finally holding our own hands behind our backs until the sun beiged the black sand, and we found a path through the panic grass leading home.

Our mother was smoking on the front stoop when we arrived. Everything about her was clenched. Smoke curled from her fingers as if they were embers and, behind us, we could feel the horizon disappear. "We didn't think . . ." we began. But before we could finish, she turned her back on us and went inside. Our mother always knew what we were going to say before we said it. We watched her disappear down the hall and realized she had nothing to give us.

That night for dinner, our mother served a new dish for our new selves: "Welsh rarebit," she said, placing a steaming yellow mess on the lazy Susan. She looked like an idea of a mother. We cried as we ate, because we thought it was rabbit—so creamy and velvet, and because there would never be enough.

The next week, want was taught in every class. In French— je veux, I want, was corrected for politesse to je voudrais, I would like, but it tasted the same in our mouths. In history, wanting was blamed for the war. In science, an experiment proved subjects who'd recently eaten salt perceived a glass of water as closer than subjects who'd just drunk to their contentment.

Since visiting the Wanting Beach, our stomachs ached
and our knees looked like faces. We woke, palms sweating, in the middle of the night; small red bumps appeared
under our shirts, ringing our waists in itch. We wanted so
much our throats burned. We wanted the big loud world
beating around us, vibrating our ribs; we wanted storms;
we wanted vistas. We wanted honey and musk; we wanted
mouthfuls of cake. We wanted gushing periods, thick eyebrows, wind chafing our faces. We wanted to rename the
animals; we wanted to lead cults. We wanted to straddle
the weak, to climb skyscrapers, and hang statues of ourselves from their towers. We wanted our hymens broken;
we wanted our profiles on coins. We wanted to lead inva-
sions. We wanted to lie down naked in the middle of the
street thrumming under the stampede of the new.

The wanting was so bright it nearly blinded us. We
swore never to want again. This quickly grew problematic:
wanting not to want. We wanted wantlessness so badly,
we gave away all our things: our rings, our mirrors, our
dog. The next day our mother left us, which we told ourselves was what we wanted, which made us angry because
we'd vowed not to want, and so we blamed ourselves. The
truth was our mother had long threatened to leave, and
her absence was marked less by its suddenness than by
how little it changed the tone of the apartment—though the
mood was perceptibly off. No one approached the stove.
No one opened a window. The kitchen grew damp and fungal. The refrigerator whistled a high-pitched trill.

In our mother's wake was a windfall of nightmares: thumbs too big for doors, legs made of lead, cars washed out to sea. And a discovery of wares—ointments and corsets, boomerangs, drapes and retractable blades. We asked ourselves what a mother was. A mother was a tree in the middle of a home. A mother was a hole where missing went. A mother was never finished—half-baked cakes, unhemmed dresses, marked catalogs for stores that no longer existed.

We were debating the relationship between wanton and want when a woman appeared in our foyer. We didn't want her there, but we didn't want her gone. She appeared in the foyer and lent it an air of formality. Where she stood, we had once had a coat-tree, a shoe rack, and an umbrella stand but soon before our mother left, she had moved them to the stoop.

"Don't you want," our mother had called from the doorway to every man who passed. It wasn't clear if she was offering the furniture or admonishing their desire. One man hefted the coat-tree like a bride over his shoulder and carried it away. A second man snatched the shoe rack, hailed a cab, and sped off. A last man set his bag of groceries in the umbrella stand, tenderly lifted it to his chest, bowed to our mother, and ambled down the sidewalk.

We remembered all this when the woman arrived in a dripping coat and rain boots, her dark hair drenched. Handshakes had never been encouraged in our family

—whether from fear of intimacy or germs, we could not say—but we nodded at the woman. "Mmmm," she hummed inside her throat as she jotted something down on her clipboard page.

It was a cool day and the woman had a slight shiver. Although we thought of offering her something, none of us did. We'd fought our own wanting so studiously, we found ourselves unsure how to meet the unspoken needs of another. Plus, we had given up entertaining. Ever since our visit to the Wanting Beach, it seemed so much could be wanted and so much could be given, that each possible guest was an undeniable argument for temptation and loss. As if, with each stranger admitted over our threshold, all the desires of all the people in the world might deluge our small apartment. And why wouldn't it be so? The world was overrun with wants.

Nevertheless, there was something affecting about the woman, so we stepped aside to admit her. She moved her eyes over the foyer, then walked forward, taking in the living room and adjacent dining area and then peering a little to the left so she could peek into the narrow kitchen.

"Mmmm," came the throat murmur again. We suspected she was there to report on our ability to care for ourselves. We were what they called "underage," though the term was questionable. After all, like the woman, we each were of an exact age, neither under nor over. Nevertheless, we had expected the arrival of someone for some

time now. The woman with the clipboard, however, made
no reference either to our youth or our motherlessness,
the latter of which we would have denied—our mother
had left no sign that she was not about to return at any
moment: her slippers beside the bed; her wallet and keys
on the counter; in the carpet, little crescents of her nails.

"I could sell your apartment," the woman said.

"No thank you," we said.

"Does it have Wi-Fi?"

"It does."

"To appeal to you, I could show you some properties
my company has recently sold for very impressive sums."

There was something of a disappointment about her,
made more disappointing by the orangey shade of lipstick
she wore on her lips and front teeth. Also, by the way
she pulled in her chin as she spoke, signaling disbelief in
her own words. She withdrew a business card from her
purse. On the card was a photograph of a similar woman
in a similar coat, with lighter hair, and the words: PIVOT
TOWARD BUYERS AND THRIVE.

"We see," we said, passing the card from one to the
other. It was wholly unimpressive.

"I just got my license," the woman said. "I have to start
somewhere."

"Not here," we said. But then we wondered if we were
beginning to want something by not wanting it. Curiosity
breeds intimacy. We blushed.

"Can you sing?"

"Can we what?"

"Do you sing together?"

"No," we said.

"You should. Group singing is easier than working out and cheaper than therapy. Singing fortifies and enriches."

Was this what they taught in real estate school? To sell something is better than to sell nothing? Could she sell us on singing? Make us the next girl group? Be our agent?

We had never before received a solicitation this professional, as we lived in a building with an off-putting facade. We were, however, accustomed by then to dodging the slew of advertisements aimed at our demographic, which claimed to have what we wanted. Our latest method was to focus instead on what we needed: twelve hundred calories and invisibility, which required neither wanting nor being wanted, respectively.

It was increasingly difficult to be girls and unwanted, but we worked at it. We bathed just enough not to give off an odor, but not enough to be fragrant. We wore mid-calf length skirts with loose-fitting tops that didn't quite match. The idea was to be asexual, uncategorizable—neither hipster nor scene, yet not so puzzling as to encourage scrutiny. When we spoke, we favored verbs and nouns, and tuned our voices slightly to the nasal. Whenever possible, we farted. We farted now.

"Mmmm," the woman hummed. It seemed to be a tic. We thought it was a clever tic for a woman to adopt, as it filled the silence and could be read as any number of virtues: a sign of approval, contentment, sympathy, or agreement.

As for a woman with a clever tic in a dripping coat offering to represent us, that was something we didn't think we needed but also something we didn't think we needed to do without, either. Particularly now that she was here in our foyer and had given us her card. The question was, did girls need representation? If so, by whom? And were we entertaining the notion of the woman with the clipboard as our representative, simply because she was the only candidate or because she was one possible older version of ourselves? Was this a problem? Might we be selling ourselves short? And what, exactly, did girls have that ought to be sold? One true fact: Her coat was dripping on our floor.

"Would you like San Carlo Rodeos? They're Italian Fritos," we surprised ourselves by asking. There was a drawer in our kitchen filled with foreign versions of American snacks. We assumed they had been a collection of our late father.

"Maybe," the woman said.

"Hang your coat in the shower. Come back next week, and we'll give you the chips."

"I'll come back tomorrow."

Clearly the woman wanted something from us. We wondered if she'd been to the Wanting Beach. Could she be our heroine? Was her wanting acceptable or inexhaustible?

"Drying takes time," we said, "and we must find the snacks and empty them into a bowl."

The woman stood in her wet boots, "Mmmm," and jotted some more notes on her clipboard paper.

"The thing is," we said, "for you to exit the foyer."

We watched her cross to the bathroom, heard her pull the shower curtain aside, and saw her reemerge in a blue dress that was short enough to show her chapped knees. We were surprised she had chapped knees on such a damp day. It added to her lack of authenticity and also caused a creeping desire to help her. Under the right circumstances, we might teach her what we'd discovered online about not wanting through meditation: *Observe the want, neither condemning nor indulging it.* We wanted her to stay. No one was to blame. We guided her out the door.

The woman's appearance and disappearance made us want our mother. *Hold the want in loving awareness.* Not the hollow mother who'd left us, but the mother she might have been had she conquered the Wanting Beach, protected by her square teeth and her deep voice and her breath that smelled of licorice and bitters. *Notice how it feels in the body.* Our necks were stiff. Our shoulders rose when we inhaled. *See how it moves and changes.* We had few clues of our mother being the way we wanted her, but there was a framed photograph in the hall of a young woman on a lawn with a book, where it seemed she once knew where she ended and others began. We could feel our hearts beat in our throats. When we reminded her of our father, she'd walk away or sometimes grab us up and kiss us. *Softly repeat the name of the want the whole time it is present until it ends.* Leonard Cohen came to mind.

We took up places around the baby grand piano and expected the song would be there—either in the form of sheet music or memory, but we located neither. One of us hummed a first note but we could not match it. The same happened when one of us hit a piano key—we were always flat.

It was a good thing, not singing. Because, really, if we'd found a melody and sung it in one voice or three-part harmony, there'd have been no telling what could have happened. As it was, we sat down and looked up at the piano's soundboard from underneath. We gripped our ankles, felt our bodies contract. Surely, we were not the only girls who would never sing. People were always losing abilities before they realized they had them, and it was nobody's fault. Least of all their own.

Instead of singing, we sat in a circle beneath the piano and invented a memory of our mother in her hair days—before the Wanting Beach—teaching us to braid: She called us into her room where she sat at her dressing table letting us practice on her own hair, which was long and dark and smooth.

Every hour until bed, we brought this scene to mind, altering it slightly and building the story into our synapses; we manipulated, recalled, rewrote. Projected memories were amended into a truth we all accepted: On school days, when we were rushing to make the bus, our mother would whistle and we'd line up in the hall to braid one another's hair, with her in the rear. Our hair was finer than our mother's and shorter, but we imitated her touch down the line: fingers pointed and strong, like rain on the puddle of our scalps. Because she taught us each a different braid, we each went to school with a different hairstyle, depending upon the order in which we stood: French, Fishtail, Halo.

"She was an exemplar," we said.

"Our succor and our champion."

"Not boys on a beach."

"Not a woman with a clipboard."

We were almost happy, then. We fell lightly into bed as if we were each a specific, answerable question.

The next morning, we slept in. The sun made its way from window to window, and we did not feel the morning's sharpness. Or we felt it, but passively, like the teeth in our mouths. We looked at one another from our pillows. We wiggled our toes. A mouse crossed the floor and stopped in our communal gaze.

When the woman appeared in the foyer again, we were in the living room comparing the flexibility of our hamstrings. As a rule, we did not compare ourselves to one another (compare and despair), but flexibility seemed an innocuous, yet necessary trait to cultivate.

People were always spraining, twisting, and breaking parts of themselves for lack of stretching. The super tore his ACL. The bus driver complained of back pain. The art teacher had tennis elbow. Only a pain-free body was a body one could deny.

"You're here for the chips," we said.

"Mmmm," she said.

We made a show of having to search for the Italian chips. In fact, we had organized the snack drawer first thing when our mother disappeared. It was both comforting and disconcerting to realize just how long packaged foods remained edible.

"Disconcerting," the woman said. "Mmmm."

We had not been aware that we'd said the adjective aloud, which was itself disconcerting but also comforting. Perhaps someone understood us.

The woman was rounder than we'd remembered. And pinker. The wet coat then might be a sort of camouflage. There was so much for a woman to cover up.

"Do you ever not wear the coat?" we asked.

"The wanting coat?" We stopped our stretching. Did she say wanting or haunting?

"Bring it to us," we said.

The woman entered the bathroom and we heard a snap and shake like a bullfighter with his cape. She reemerged wearing her dry coat. We surrounded her, feeling for pockets, but there were none. We decided she must not have said wanting, but taunting.

"Here's a list of common emotional triggers—" she handed us her clipboard, "unmet needs people react to. Which are yours?"

"None," we said, stepping back, not looking at her list.

"Mine are 'Acknowledgment' and 'Being Liked.'"

"Actually," we said, looking now, "'Safety' and 'Being Right.'"

"Mmmm."

Uncomfortable silence ensued. We felt it in our chests. We stretched our shoulders wide, looked at the door and then at one another.

We remembered the snacks and brought them out in a bowl decorated like a Holstein cow; our parents had acquired a large selection of mismatched crockery from years of living communally in various ideological settings.

"Did I hear you sing earlier?"

"No," we said.

"*I have heard the mermaids singing, each to each. I do not think that they will sing to me.*"

"What are you after?" we asked, feeling an agitation in our legs, like a low electrical current.

"Same as you," the woman said, "hunger without fear." She was hunched over the corn snacks, smelling, but not eating them. "In the meantime," she lifted her head from the bowl, "I have more apartments to approach."

That evening, we found the woman's pen in the bathroom. It must have fallen out when she'd played the torero. A gold-nibbed fountain pen with a sandalwood barrel, it was not the type of pen we could keep without guilt. We thought we'd pay a visit to the real estate agency's office and ask for the woman. We prepared as best we could for any eventuality—practiced everything from rolling our r's to roundhouse kicks. We surprised ourselves with the variety of our as-of-yet unused talents. In the morning, we drank green tea. Ate a handful of roasted pepitas. Sometimes our apartment offered up nutrition, other times, only stink bugs.

We walked single file through the open office door of Your Realtors. We pondered the name and found it wanting. Sometimes it was easier to find things outside of ourselves that wanted. Sharing a sense of deficiency with the entire known world made it less lonely to be away from home.

There were women at desks who looked up at our arrival, then back down again. Was it because we were youngish? Palish? Smelled of nothing? The woman from the business card was not among the so-called realtors. We found the term laughable as there'd been little that had felt real about the woman who'd visited us, particularly now that she was not to be found in her purported place of business.

"May I help you?" one of the women finally said. We tried to imagine ourselves as grown women: not wanting to help but pretending to. We would be smarter than these women; we would not be in blouses behind desks. But who would we be? And where were the women who demonstrated anything at all that did not look like a euphemism for woman? Outside a truck backed up and the shop filled with its warning beeps; a chair squeaked; a phone rang. We spun in our sneakers and left. As soon as we'd exited the agency, we spotted our realtor about a block away, her back to us, standing at a bus stop in the coat. We hurried toward her.

"You left this," we said, holding out the pen.

The woman turned around. She looked grateful and reached out to take the pen, but it was not her. Embarrassed, we pocketed the pen, and pretending we'd just heard our names called, ran across the street and down the block.

And because our legs were already running, and running felt like what our legs were meant for, we ran on. We watched ourselves flash by in store windows. Saw it clearly: the want in our eyes, pointless and burning, greedy and curious. We told ourselves we were young and that was to be expected. Wants might arrive, but we did not have to serve them. We picked up speed. We ran past children climbing fences. We reminded ourselves: Want would always be dangerous, would bring us to the attention of the authorities. We ran past men at tables, hunched and gesticulating. We sprinted faster down the road, past beggars in hats, past preachers with fliers. We

bit the insides of our cheeks. We tried to reason with ourselves: treat want as pilot light—flame enough to get up in
the morning but not enough to combust. By the time our
mother left, she was burning blue.

Still, we felt our want building and filling us, con-
centrating deep in our girl bodies, until we became mag-
nets with vector fields, pointed and irresistible. Want as
weapon, want as shield—attracting all that was deprived,
repelling all that was obliged. Our sight grew keen and
panoramic; we could see ahead to the shore and the ocean
beyond and also behind us, to the line of people some distance back, now following. Our clothes grew heavy and
peeled off as we slowed to a walk, breathing deeply. We
passed our building and continued to the end of the road.
New words formed on our lips. Seedlings sprouted from
our footprints. We were suddenly aware of the muscles in
our arms; the day turned a new color.

Something powerful took hold of us: a want so strong
we were temporarily paralyzed. We shared a look that
said we all wanted the same thing, and we all wished one
of us would do what we all wanted, but none of us wanted
to do it. We were afraid. Then something pushed us—a
gust of wind or a feather, and we headed forward to the
Wanting Beach.

A hot breeze lifted off the beach, and we suddenly
recalled the list of needs that could be unmet. Recalling the needs gave them presence in the afternoon heat.
Needs and wants began to confuse themselves, and the air

felt tangled and thick. We brought our focus to the earth, passed the pen from one to the other, cutting our names into the sand. When we finished, we threw the pen into the sea. Then we squatted, leaned forward, and lowered our heads. At first our arms hung like garlands around us. Then slowly we swung them forward and back, digging wings into the sand. The surf filled our wing molds with foam, and we had never felt so ready. The beach was dark and steaming. The sky was low.

i YOU SHE

I WAS TOLD BY a bald man with no books left in him, never to write in the second person and also never to write a story about a writer.

You were strolling alongside a river, which was a kind of story that meandered, and his prohibition stuck to you like a burr.

She was, of course, a writer.

I told the bald man I would write a story in the first, second, *and* third person about a writer who fucked a visiting professor, to which he shrugged and said, "Sounds cute."

You loved cute: scars in the shape of smiles, windigos, your little round turds after you drank too much.

So, she and the visiting bald professor went out and drank too much and fucked—all for the sake of the story.

I was behaving badly, and my mother was worried, and my only friend said, "Go to China where you won't know anyone, and you can teach kindergarten and get your shit together."

You believed you could be a different person in a different country.

She asked the bald professor for money for an abortion—she lied; of course she wasn't pregnant—and used it to buy a one-way ticket to Shanghai.

I was unqualified for the kindergarten gig, which I got easily, and the job paid the rent but not much else, so when, in an online chat group for expats, I found an ad: SEEKING WESTERN ACTORS TO PERFORM AS BAND MEMBERS AT COMPANY OPENING, I applied.

Unlike Mandarin, impersonation you understood.

The next week she earned 1,000 yuan for standing on a stage with other "musicians" and pretending to play the drums as a member of Heartbreakers, "America's Top Country Music Band," while canned music blasted and libations flowed.

I thought it might make an honest woman of me to be paid to be a fraud.

You quickly fell for Aimée, as her name instructed, the French singer of Heartbreakers who didn't know how to sing and couldn't speak English, and who'd been doing this—pretending to be the singer in an American country band—for a year.

In her high school-level French, she wooed Aimée who smiled and led her on, but who, she suspected, only liked her because of her closeness with Bart, the keyboardist.

I taught my kindergarten students "Head Shoulders Knees and Toes," which impressed their parents and made me think of Aimée, whose body parts I longed to memorize.

For you, unrequited love felt like having your cake and eating it too.

Besides the kindergarten hours and the Heartbreakers hours, she spent occasional hours at modeling jobs.

Once, I modeled for a breast pump company, demonstrating the buttons, then holding another woman's baby so close he latched on to my nipple.

You mentioned the nipple incident casually to Aimée, hoping she too would find you delectable.

There was a reason it was called *making* love she knew, she who made her life over and over again from scratch.

I entertained Aimée with details about Bart, the keyboardist who could not play the keyboards but was fluent
in Putonghua and had a part-time job as assistant to the
director of a government-backed firm he knew nothing
about, and Aimée laughed when I described to her his
business card, possibly because my French was such that
I may have called the business card his affairs map.

You played dumb and then wondered why people
treated you like you were stupid.

Inspired by the Chinese rent-a-foreigner practice, she
fantasized about renting what she needed to create a strik-
ing impression for Aimée's sake—a Rottweiler, a doting
auntie, an entourage.

I was helpless around Aimée—the press of her palms
around a cup, the angle of her knees in her jeans, the humid
wind smell of her; her nearness caused a disturbance like
an accordion being fingered and squeezed inside my chest.

Bart made frequent use of the expression, *of course*—
"Of course Aimée is teaching me French," "Of course my
boss is gay"—which, of course, felt like small muggings,
because to you, nothing was ever self-evident.

She could not turn off the voice in her head that said
something was waiting for her just around the corner.

I tried to lure Aimée over to my apartment by arranging a
threesome with Bart, but he had to accompany the director of his firm to a business dinner, and later, when he

reported the dinner was très amusant, I had to admit it sounded so, as all he was required to do was eat, drink, and be exotic, a familiar task for a Jew from Baltimore.

Your kindergarten students enjoyed making little turkeys out of their hands, and when you asked them what they were thankful for, they said you.

If only she and Aimée could have met as kindergarteners, sitting next to one another holding hands, two little turkey hands, fluttery and ready to fly.

I was finding it hard to be a person, i.e., hard to write home about, hard to sit with, hard to believe.

You thought Aimée was your meant-to-be, as you had trouble understanding her, and wasn't love always a matter of translation.

She learned from her kindergarteners the importance of consistent routines and rules, so three nights a week, she met Aimée and Bart for drinks which she bought, and she made a rule of only staring at Aimée for ten seconds at a time, after which she looked away and pinched herself.

I spent so much time with Aimée and Bart, I began to think Heartbreakers was a real band.

By then, you'd realized even the act of dressing was the creation of a persona.

The three bandmates supported and undermined one another and left everyone else out, which was a definition of close, she was sure.

One night I went over to Aimée's house to surprise her with a bottle of wine and found Bart on the couch in his underwear.

Along with your kindergarten students, you napped in the middle of the day, and were soon secure enough in your job to dream.

The next day she dreamed she was rolling a barrel along a beach and as the barrel rolled, it imprinted words onto the sand—WALK ALL OVER ME WHY DON'T YOU, and as she rolled the barrel, she walked on the words and Aimée lay topless on the beach, watching her and smiling a smile that said either, "You are adorable" or "You are laughable," and the more she walked over her own words, the worse she was making it, and Aimée lay in the sun until her skin began to peel and underneath Aimée's peeling skin was another layer of skin, and she kept rolling the barrel and walking on her words and sweating in the sun, unable to get out of the scene gracefully, and then she heard screaming children, her kindergarteners, in the water, because she'd let her guard down, they couldn't swim and now they were drowning, and Aimée was frowning, and all the lifeguards were bald men, turning their backs and shrugging, but then Bart came running down the beach carrying his keyboard-shaped surfboard, and Aimée cheered and plunged into the water after him, and she thought they were going to save her by saving the drowning children but instead Aimée and Bart just rode away on the waves.

When I finally understood Aimée was only using me for my drinks and my adoration, I exorcised her by writing a play in which Bart was my husband, and Aimée was his lover, and all three parts were played by me.

You nearly lost your mind, but instead found your creative power.

On a long strip of paper, she listed everything she'd ever been told she could not do, then stuffed the scroll inside a helium balloon, and let it go.

CORPSE POSE

MY MOTHER WAS AN anal-retentive neurotic all about the Purell and the egg-free batter licking, so when I dropped dead while teaching a yoga class at age twenty-five, she would have none of it. It was her yoga studio and a grieving mother with a buried daughter did not suit. She laid my body out on the instructor's dais and combed my long hair and filed my square nails, both of which kept growing though I did not open my eyes.

She believed herself to be a good person, but my mother was relieved I was gone. (She'd never gotten over having to care for someone else just when she'd finally come into her own.) So, my mother navigated the cognitive dissonance thus: She convinced herself it was better for me that I was dead—no more psychoanalysis, no more blind dates with charming narcissists who had projective identification issues, no more apple cider vinegar cleanses. Ironically, she was right. But not for the reasons she told herself.

What my mother didn't know about death: There was a clarity to being dead. The thick glass between the world and me melted away. Je pense donc je ne suis plus. I think because I'm no longer. No longer prone to the distractions of the body, my mind at last was free. Death offered an integrity that life could not. In life, I'd been obsessed with my body. Either its improvement—burpees, brow gel, or its discomforts—PMS, paper cuts. Dead, I had use for neither hypochondria nor the latest self-help webinars. It was a relief no longer worrying about halter bras or halitosis. Even when it's short, life is long.

It helped that I was freed of embodied memories. My hands forgot gripping. My closed mouth was just another curtained entrance. Even my face could not remember how to grin in discomfort or tense at a compliment. So, it was true: Arrange your face in a relaxed position and inner stillness followed. I was all presence. At last, I could be the introvert that I was. And there was nothing but time. Time for the slow spread of day across the studio's gray walls; time for the flow of traffic outside the window as it swished the rain-slicked street.

The shock of being dead is that your sense-gates open. Everything opaque becomes apparent and the world offers itself to your third eye. Thanks to the ajna chakra I perceived everything around me; the world rushed in and death was a coming home. I had vision without any of the ugly senses— sight but no taste; hearing but no feeling. And the best part of being dead? No more smells. Everything smelled when I was alive—the world was an assault of odor—breath, sewage, sweat, dog, mulch, exhaust. . . . Now the studio could fill with overheating bodies, the Chinese takeout in the storefront below could fry onions, the oil truck could pump its vaporous delivery into the building, and I was at peace. Ah-ooh-mm. Nothingness. It was a beautiful thing.

I dropped dead, and the transformation was like eating a poem. Jackal's benediction in the forest of the heart. Language made fresh tunnels in me like worms in compost. I was a stilled hammock, cupped with shadow and atmosphere. A flower plucked, drying in the sun.

Twice daily my mother brushed my skin with sisal bristles, so I remained radiant and supple. When it became apparent that my menses would continue regardless of my expired state, she brought the stash of sanitary pads from the bathroom to the yoga dais and changed them between classes. She didn't have to plan. Once I was dead, my periods followed the moon strictly.

At first, the students were spooked. They walked into class, spied me lying there on my mat unmoving in my harem pants and swing tank, and giggled nervously. My mother taught her classes—sometimes standing in front of me, sometimes walking around the room—and because she was their teacher and because she scared them more than my prone body did, they soon acclimated to the setup.

My mother was a presence, not only in the yoga studio, but in the town. She owned the studio, the building which housed the studio, and the building around the corner where her world-famous yoga-ware company was based and in which she employed three-quarters of the town. She knew the entire police force by name. In all but appointment, she ran the PTA. There were students in her classes who hated yoga but were afraid of what my mother would say or do if they didn't show up. She kept the synovial fluid of the town's population flowing whether they liked it or not.

"Bring your inner gaze to your midbrain," my mother told her classes, glancing from me to them. She found inspiration in my prone state. "Enter the yoga of suspended awareness. Can you imagine controlling your life force?" On her own, between classes, she sat steadily beside me working on her pratyahara, withdrawing from the senses. My mother was competitive, and my youth and beauty had been hard on her. In middle age she had thickened and creased, and any attention I received, she received as inattention to herself. So, as I lay immobile on the stage of her yoga studio, she took up the challenge to meet and surpass my internal state with the perfection of her own samadhi.

Still, in the beginning, surrender was an adjustment. There were days I would have liked to have gotten up, taken a walk by the river. Particularly at sunset, when the room filled with a reddish glow and a hush came over the studio, and I knew something beautiful was dying outside and I could no longer participate. I would have liked a fire in the fireplace; I would have liked to read.

Anyway, one can adapt to just about anything. If neuroscientists could swap people into different bodies through experiments with mannequins and helmet cameras—a woman into a man, a slim man into an obese man, a man with three arms, a woman with a foot-long nose— and they all adjusted, so could I. And I did. In fact, if you'd asked me after the first few weeks, I'd have said, best day of my life was my death. I used to be self-conscious—*Do my bangs make me look stupid? If I look you in the eye, will you think I want to fuck you?* No more. I never much liked myself. In fact, when I was alive, I saw myself as a perpetual Under Development Work-In-Progress. I wasn't nice enough; I wasn't authentic enough. I only looked out for myself; I put everybody else first. I wasn't generous; I was a pushover. I had no style; I was always looking for attention. It was confusing. It was exhausting. Then I died and, after a short acclimation, it was like hitting the happiness jackpot.

FIVE PROVEN HAPPINESS HACKS:

1. Friends & Family: According to a study in the *Journal of Socio-Economics*, regularly seeing friends and family was worth $97,265 a year. I was with my mother forty hours a week and the studio filled daily with regulars. What's more, another study showed the clearest benefit of social relationships came from helping others. By just lying there, I was a constant reminder of the preciousness of life. Yogis could repeat all there *is* is the present moment all day long, but nothing was as puissant as a baby-faced dead girl to bring the message home. Plus, my former students still posted on my Facebook page, reread my blog (EyeBow2U), and rewatched my Vlogs (Yoga vs. Life). I was the gift that kept on giving.

2. 57 Degrees: According to research published by the American Meteorological Society, happiness is maximized at 57 degrees. Located in an old warehouse building, the studio had huge, leaky windows, and I was lucky enough to be laid out under the leakiest of them all. In winter, even when the heat was clicking and cranking, my body benefited from a steady, bracing breeze. Also, to preserve me—and her bottom line—my mother turned the heat down between classes. Summertime the studio stayed cool from a combination of shade and the pittas in the classes constantly asking to turn up the AC and fans.

3. Light: Sunlight brightens mood. My apartment was dark and had shades. The studio was a prism for moving light—silver to yolk to fever to steel.

4. Citrus: For dozens of years, International Flavors & Fragrances, Inc. measured the effects of aromas on emotions through mood mapping. Citrus scents were shown to lift mood. When I was alive, I was allergic to perfume and had to air out the studio after Marjorie's class because she wore orange jasmine essential oil on her pressure points. When I died, she took over my classes and, now, there was citrus positivity five times a week where I lay. To cell physiologists aware of the numerous olfactory receptors in skin, the perks of aromatherapy for a picky anosmic should not surprise.

5. Touch: A study from UNC–Chapel Hill found human touch is essential to happiness, and just as one may benefit from odor without the ability to smell, one may benefit from touch without being able to feel. My mother read an article about the far-reaching effects of touch and booked me a weekly Thai massage. George was a small brown-skinned ageless man with close-cropped hair and muscular hands. When he arrived for the first appointment, my mother launched into an explanation of the situation. George cut her off with a quiet pressure on her shoulder.

"I have hospice training," he said. He opened his rubber massage mat and placed me face down onto it. He then proceeded to pull, stretch, and rock me. It was novel not to worry about sexual feelings or bodily embarrass-ments—there was a small release of flatulence, which George gamely ignored. When it came time to turn me face up, he lifted me from the waist and spun me around. I remained clothed, so there was none of the usual awk-wardness of under-the-sheet flashing. George's profes-sionalism was impeccable, which was a first for me, and a little insulting. No flirtatious banter, no sly brush of hand over breast. He massaged me supine, prone, side-lying, and seated. He pulled my fingers, cracked my toes, walked on my back, all the while accompanying his rhythm with a steady monologue.

Over the weeks I learned things about George even his priest didn't know: He called his legislators every morning and wrote a letter to the president every day expressing measured outrage in memes he scoured from the internet and printed on recycled paper. He counted his steps to be sure he went to bed on an even number. Older women's ankles made him miss his aunt. He recited the same joke aloud in his car before every job. He kept his dried, used contact lenses in a baby food jar on the windowsill. He acted out the scenes of mystery novels as he read them.

Things continued in the pure, timeless way of death for me while all around, life went on, and soon it was approaching the shortest day of the year. On that day, it so happened that a man came to the studio to sample a trial class. When he walked into the room, he was so taken by the vision of my beautiful, lifeless body, he had to take off his Tom Ford green frame eyeglasses so as not to stare. After class, he waited outside the studio for me to exit. When I didn't, he waited until the last class of the day had come and gone, and after my mother turned off the lights and locked the door, he broke into the studio through an unlocked bathroom window.

"Hello?" he called into the darkness. "Are you there?" When no one answered, he opened the door to the studio and stood staring at me from across the room. First, he cleared his throat. He turned the lights on and quickly off. Then, he approached me, placed his hands on my shoulders, and gave me a shake. When I did not respond, he slapped my face. Finally, he leaned his head down over my lips and breathed into my mouth. With each of his breaths, my lungs filled with air and my chest rose. This seemed to be enough for him. Or, I should say, too much. He pulled my shirt over my head and cupped my breasts in his hands. Soon he was astride me. He pushed my waistband to my knees and forced himself inside me. He growled softly as he moved, and toward the end, called out, "I love you!"

Had I been alive, I might have swapped out my wardrobe for shapeless, unfitted clothes and shaved off all my hair. I might have written a book of harrowingly deft poems channeling a Pre-Raphaelite Parisian prostitute or become an installation artist known for panoramic friezes made of lace from the underwear of human trafficking victims. As it was, I was dead and had neither the ability nor the need to do a thing.

The next day my mother found me as I'd been left: hair in my mouth, shirt over my nose, ripped thong. She cleaned and re-dressed me, mumbled "Om shanti shanti shanti" under her breath, and carried on.

There followed a period of low class attendance, which may have been a reflection of my mother's state of mind (tamas), or it may have been just the cold days and long nights. In the past, this lull in business would have meant endless arguments with my mother. She was a stress arguer. I was a stress ruminator. And while being dead was stress-free, I could still pick up the tension she emitted.

While alive, I'd read about Cleve Backster, world expert on the use of polygraphs, who experimented with plants, bacteria, eggs, sperm, and white cells from the mouth to prove they all showed signs of connected intelligence: When the sperm donor inhaled amyl nitrate, his sperm in the next room went wild; when a Pearl Harbor vet went home to watch a TV show on Japanese air strikes, his white cheek cells miles away reacted to the threat.

So, yes, I picked up on my mother's slow-season stress. And yes, because I'd been a habitual stress ruminator, ideas arrived like cud those quiet days.

Almost anything could set off an idea-churn—a flicker of light, an overheard comment. One of my former students lost thirty-five pounds, and when her friend complimented her new body as they returned their bolsters to the pile near my feet, she confided her fear that she wouldn't be able to keep off the weight. The idea—weight loss vs. maintenance—led to a good week of chewing: Why were diets so good at getting weight off but so bad at keeping it off? Wasn't it the same skill: Do eat this; don't eat that? Why did the average woman spend thirty-one years of her life on a diet? What if it weren't the thin body slimmers craved, but the goal of the thin body? What if you could harness that goal seeking? Raise people up the evolutionary ladder from wanting a thin body to wanting a better world? Like Maimonides' Eight Levels of Tzedakah (one year at Shari Tefilah Hebrew School before my mother became Buddhist). Could this change the world? To this dead girl, it sure seemed it could. It was odd having all the time in the world to pick up on what was going on, but no ability to do anything about it.

Astounding is the power of a brain, even a dead brain. One day my mother gave a dharma talk on the practice of surrender in which she led everyone in a guided meditation. "Bring your attention to your heart center. What is the quality of your heart? Is there constriction? Imagine you can see from your heart. Imagine your heart is a flower bud. Inhale into the bud of your heart. Exhale and allow the bud to open. One out-breath at a time. See the bud of your heart open slowly, gently, into a beautiful flower, petal by petal, breath by breath . . ."

Everyone was doing it. The room filled with carbon dioxide with each exhalation. In a matter of minutes, there was a crowded sense of flowers, a funerary overflow of conjured bouquets, and people began rocking queasily on their cushions. Someone coughed. Someone else gagged. One woman rose from her mat hunched and slipped quickly out of the room. Another followed, even more quickly, hand over mouth. My mother rose and opened the window. This caused more agitation in the group. A man opened the door that led to the balcony. Soon flies were buzzing around my head.

In the end, it was a thanatology student who happened to be in the class that day who identified the problem. She leaned toward my mother and whispered, "Carrion flower," with a nod in my direction. Apparently, my mother's guided meditation had conjured a species of *Amorphophallus titanum* in me that, predictably, emitted the odor of rotting flesh. Quickly my mother switched the visualization to a breezy white sand beach, and the class resumed.

Snowplows scraped and salted streets, then the white-breasted nuthatch began its nasal call, and then I was showing. At first, my mother tried to hide it, rearranged my top to distract from the small bump, but this was useless, and she quickly switched her approach to sevā and began to pay me extra attention—rubbing my lips with expensive balms, acupressure on my hands and feet, reading stories to me between classes.

In the second week of spring, the thanatology student returned to class, and after wiping sweat from her brow, she asked my mother's permission to use me as a case study for her final course requirement: Independent Applied Research Project—Death, a Near-Life Experience.

"With my pre-certification, if I stand watch over her body, there will be no need to worry about the authorities," she said. To my mother, the threat was both vague and laughable. Nevertheless, she agreed. My mother craved a break. When she was pregnant with me, she later told me (chin bowed, hands over her sacral chakra), she wasn't ready to be a mother; when I turned twenty, she asked me how I could be so old when she was so young. When I was alive, I interfered with my mother's life. Dead, I did as well. So, my mother left the vigil to the thanatology student, telling herself she was doing the intense young woman a favor.

The woman, Sylvie, was indeed intense. But not so young. She was, in fact, forty-nine and treating herself with gene therapy to reverse her aging. Every morning since she was twenty-five, she injected into her thigh the spun cells of the *Turritopsis nutricula*, a small species of jellyfish known to be biologically immortal. Sylvie had long silken hair. Her skin was luminous to the point of near transparency. She moved on the yoga mat with the fluidity of water. When my mother left for the day, Sylvie took up her post. She sat in meditation using my whirlpool-shaped outie navel as her drishti. "Om Namah Shivaya," she chanted, and a swirl of energy swept the room like seagrass.

By the sixth day of Sylvie's ceaseless attention, people began to notice something crucial had shifted. Another student, a regular at the studio for years, arrived to class with a basket slung over her elbow. After unrolling her mat, she laid her offerings at my feet—heirloom seeds in a dozen cups that had the quality of filling the air with a sense of childlike awe. My mother reacted immediately. She told Sylvie enough was enough. "Go home; take a break; feed your fish." My mother's agitation did not faze Sylvie, who only smiled back. A subtle, muscle-less smile that caused my mother to turn away and float out of the room.

By the end of that week, my body was cocooned in a pile of alms from the community at large: pizza delivery boy (six-pack of beer), parking enforcement officer (jars of ointment), energy bar rep (carton of oatmeal), CSA organizer (loaves of chocolate chip pumpkin bread), receptionist (deck of Queen of Hearts cards), mother of receptionist (drawer sachets), and nearly every student (marbles, eyeliner, pocketknives . . .) paid his or her respects.

It was during Sylvie's vigil that she and George first met. Initially, he was against her being in the room during the massage. "This is an act of solo service," he said. "Only caregiver and care-receiver," but he was not impervious to the joy induced by the citrus stem cell serum she wore, and when Sylvie replied with her watery smile, he simply began. She fell for the way his hands fixed my body while his feet massaged it. He fell for her fierce gelatinousness.

Soon George was chauffeuring Sylvie back and forth from the studio to her, or more often his, place.

Forty weeks to the day of the break-in, my water broke. It was at the end of one of my mother's advanced Vinyasa Flow classes—"Can you make your push-ups exercises in weightlessness." And because it was a slow leak, she dabbed with her sock at the puddle spreading slowly over the dais, draped a blanket over my lap, and continued through the purifying sweat, the even, deep breathing, and the guided meditation to Savasana, Corpse Pose, Namaste.

I remained deathly throughout the labor, which was fine with my mother. She managed the whole bloody affair with the assistance of Sylvie's unsettling adaptability and her own competence and expertise. At the start of my third trimester, my mother had bought a stethoscope on eBay, and when my contractions began, she tracked them methodically recording my labor's phases. She placed me in Utthita Balasana, extended child pose, and Sylvie kneaded my lower back. When I was in transition, they carried me to the tub my mother had rented for the water birth to minimize the baby's traumatic change of environment. When labor briefly stalled, Sylvie palpitated my belly as my mother repeatedly pulled on my arms and lifted my dead weight from a prone position to one in which I sat up with every delayed contraction until my body's sit-ups pushed the baby out. With her usual efficiency, my mother suctioned the little boy's nostrils clear, and he cried. Just as they'd taken my body from the tub and begun to dry me, my uterus convulsed again, and Sylvie caught a baby girl. Twins. Each woman lifted a newborn to one of my breasts where the babies nursed vigorously. "Compassionate presence," Sylvie wrote in her master's thesis, "leads to surprising end-of-life beginnings."

At first, my mother acted as if nothing had changed. The twins slept in clear hospital-grade bassinets at my side. Classes were taught. Diapers were changed. Soon, however, the infants became distracting. They were ideal babies—content to stare at their open futures with undisturbed eyes—but their very placidity quickly became their liability. No one could resist them. Classes were overbooked with students sidetracked from their asanas by an overpowering urge to be near the burbling babies. Everyone wanted to hold the infants, to smell their scalps, to swaddle and rock them. At the beginning of class, when the instructors invited the class to set their intentions, students offered to bathe the twins, to knit them hats, to sing to them. Finally, claiming it was for the protection of her grandchildren's undeveloped immune systems, my mother relocated the babies to the back studio reserved for private sessions where Sylvie and the receptionist alternated babysitting. Soon the infants were used to feeding only between classes and the days' schedule was allowed to proceed.

Sylvie continued her inquisition over my body for the final weeks of her research project. After the birth, she took to lugging her harp into the studio and singing songs based on observations of my physiology and the interpersonal dynamics she witnessed around me. Her music brought more life to my death. My mother could not organize fast enough to keep the gifts—blankets, bags of onesies, books, booties, blocks—brought by my (and now my children's) devotees from accumulating beyond the windowsill meditation altars. By the time the babies were a month old, a half-dozen twin strollers were blocking the entrance to the door.

And there was another problem. My mother noticed George's interest in Sylvie and was hurt. She had told herself the small man was surely homosexual as a way to defend against his lack of interest in her. When it became clear that George was not unaffected by female charm, my mother took it personally that he had not given her a second look. That a dead girl and a pale thanatologist were getting more love than she was, was temporarily too much for her. Claiming it was in protest of the elections, she shut the studio and donated all the detritus of devotion to the local food pantry and children's charity. She gave Sylvie the key and told her if she wanted to continue to use me for her research, she would need to take responsibility for the babies for a while as well. No doubt eager for the chance to test George's paternal instincts, Sylvie agreed.

"Take care," my mother said to me as she shut the door behind herself and set off for two weeks of chocolate-making workshops with raw, local cacao at a yoga teachers' retreat in Costa Rica. My mother departed, safe in the assumption that the babies would be cared for, and I would go nowhere.

I was not, however, left alone. After Sylvie and George left, taking the babies and a supply of milk my mother had pumped from me and stored in the small freezer in the office, the man who had broken into the studio returned. Every night thereafter, he brought a different quote from Rumi. Each night the result was the same: "Love is a river. Drink from it," and his lips were on mine. "When love itself comes to kiss you, don't hold back," and my legs were spread. "How can there be weariness when passion is present?" and he was pumping away.

Each night he began more diffident and ended more desperate. On the fourteenth night, convinced he'd heard me speak, he pressed his ear to my throat, pried my mouth open, and quickly fell asleep slumped over my bare chest. When my mother arrived at 6 a.m. to open the studio and resume her business, she found him there and thought he too was dead. The police arrived and asked if she wanted to press charges. It was not clear if they meant breaking and entering or necrophilia. By then the man was again muttering, this time Khalil Gibran: "Where are you, my beloved? Do you hear my weeping from beyond the ocean? Do you understand my need? Do you know the greatness of my patience?"

Instead of charges, my mother saw an opportunity. She summoned a justice of the peace to marry us. In that same

Journal of Socio-Economics study that valued the happiness of connection with friends, a happy marriage was worth $105,000 a year. My value had increased, and my mother could finally pass responsibility for me from next-of-kin to spouse. Announcing it was for our privacy, she locked me and the newly returned and fattened babies in the back studio, transferring the key from Sylvie to my husband. No longer needing to break in, he made a marriage bed of mats and blankets and bolsters and blocks and for a week or so, came and went in typical husbandly fashion, making love to my body, occasionally tickling the children.

Meanwhile, for her work in the field, Sylvie received the Elisabeth Kübler-Ross Prize. With the help of the monetary award, Sylvie and George found themselves in a position to act upon a dream heretofore unspoken: to move to Alaska. At a sober meeting with my mother and her son-in-law over herbal tea and vegan shortbread, the luck-struck pair offered to adopt the twins and raise them, "in a well-developed homeschool system and the best stargazing environment on the planet." My mother and husband were only too happy to oblige.

Happy endings, however, are complicated to pull off. The two-week closing of the studio had had an unexpected result: No one came back. The closure broke the spell of devotion, first to my mother, then to me.

After the honeymoon phase wore off, my husband did not return. It was my mother and me, alone again. It was quiet and strange. My mother continued her practice and left the doors open, secure in the belief that people would come again—new people who moved up from the city and didn't know her or me or the story of my life after death. In preparation, she rigged a funnel and drain for my periods and finally left me alone in the small studio behind the locked door. At last, I seemed to her the perfect daughter—self-sufficient and safe.

I heard her playing her singing bowl, but the sound was small and far-off. The heat hissed, and I could sense something beginning to rot.

THE FUTURE WAS VAGINA FORWARD

I.

ONE DAY IN A hot dry summer, I listed my vagina on Airbnb. I filled in my details, specified my policies, uploaded my photos, and my listing went live. It was official: I was a private person with a public property.

In short order, I received numerous inquiries involving time-consuming Q&As:

"I know you say no pets, but would you accept a small therapy dog?" No.

"If I paid extra, would you reconsider your prohibition against children?" No.

"I think you're too pricey for me, if you come down LMK."

"Could you elaborate on your cleaning procedures?"

Eventually, I was able to accept my first proper guest.

Larry was a slight, middle-aged man of uncertain nationality who was in and out in a fraction of the time he'd booked and left a five-star review highlighting my "soft, warm soundproof curtains." Larry was the ideal guest—neat, quiet, courteous, energy-conserving, and fragrance-free—who fluffed the couch pillows on his way out and left a thank-you note by the door.

The next day, I made certain necessary changes in my life: turned my bed to face east, unsubscribed from LinkedIn, became a freegan (procuring dinner from the dumpster outside Whole Foods where cases of arugula could be found, along with day-old bread and a good deal of portabella mushrooms).

I read a message board for Airbnb hosts and learned that the safety of my guests was my responsibility, so I bought a carbon monoxide detector, a fire extinguisher, a first aid kit, and a liter-sized bottle of hand sanitizer. I drew, laminated, and posted on the back of my door a detailed layout of my vagina with a compass in one corner showing north with the letter N and little red arrows indicating the exit route. Next, I consulted a tax lawyer. She informed me that as long as I documented and kept all receipts, I could write off everything, from the bundle of spare toothbrushes to the extra coffee filters to my Netflix subscription. "Of course," she added, "you'll also be able to deduct a portion of the depreciation of your vagina."

My second renter was called Lisa. She'd asked if I provided breakfast, so I'd bought a box of kosher berry toaster pastries and a pint of freshly squeezed orange juice. She nodded when she saw them on the counter. With Lisa, I could think and feel exactly what she was experiencing the moment she experienced it. In the past, this might have been overwhelming and caused me to offer her my vagina indefinitely, however, this time, I did not. I wrote a starred guest review in which I mentioned Lisa's punctuality and excellent communication and included a private comment thanking her for her patient suggestions regarding my vagina's accessibility. She used a wheelchair, and according to her recommendations, I moved plates and cups to the lower cabinets, popped the table up on casters, cleared a thirty-two-inch pathway from door to bed, and purchased fold-up, telescopic ramps and a set of suction grab bars.

II.

I didn't like to talk about my vagina but if the subject came up, I'd say something like how super fun it was at age whatever to realize I was female. I tried to think about my vagina as either a vagina of the past or a vagina of the future.

On rare occasions, the word vagina sounded beautiful to me, but even then, at first it sounded bad, like an aftertaste, only before, and not a taste but a sound—vagina had a beforesound that made me wince a little prior to naming it.

I was not alone but I felt like I was.

My vagina was a metaphor but also a real thing that smelled and farted and squirted and contracted and released and sang and overate and wept and slept like everything and everyone else. I liked to remind those who relied on statistics that the average human had half a vagina, which was only sort of a joke. Turned out I didn't so much not want to talk about my vagina as not want to talk about anything *but* my vagina.

I was a virgin when my vagina first spoke to me: *This is Vagina, I am currently unable to take your call; I am either away from my body or on a bike.*

My vagina was the pink elephant in the room, the thing I always thought about once I realized I wasn't supposed to, which was when I was five years old and greeted my parents' dinner guests by lifting my skirt, dropping my panties, and introducing them to my vagina, the name of which I'd just learned, and instead of the expected, "nice to meet you, Vagina," the man dinner guest had looked away, and the woman dinner guest had turned the color of her scarf, and my mother had yanked up my panties so hard their rough lace burned me from ankle to crotch. If only this were a world where people said vagina all the time like they said car or weather or Tuesday or dear: What kind of a world would that be? A world where Big Pharma was a hangar-sized apothecary brimming with tinctures and vitamins and herbs, where suppression required a therapist, not a poll watcher, and the only thing captured was carbon.

Time for some math: One vagina equaled an approach; two vaginas equaled a lecture; three vaginas equaled a joke; four or more vaginas equaled a law.

I wanted to change my life from my vagina outward. I cried a little when I thought that.

My vagina needed staff—therapist, publicist, decorator, lawyer, personal shopper, accountant, cook, but I could only afford one, so I had to choose wisely. I interviewed them together in my living room, asking them each what they would bring to the table.

> *Therapist:* I listen. When your vagina speaks, I hear it. When your vagina is silent, I interpret.
> *Publicist:* The image of your vagina is up to the people who control that image. I am that person. I can control the narrative.
> *Decorator:* The skills to transform your vagina into the outward expression of your truest self. Discounts with vendors. Excellent references.
> *Lawyer:* Thousands of hours representing the interests of your vagina. I will work tirelessly to win your vagina the settlements it deserves.
> *Personal Shopper:* Whatever your vagina needs, I've taken care of it *before* you recognize the need.

Accountant: Your vagina should not have to worry about regulations or compliance. I'll protect your vagina's assets while keeping your vagina out of the sights of the government.

Cook: Nothing fazes me—late hours, noise, odors— I'm your man.

I thanked them for their time but decided instead on a DIY approach. With the saved salary, I bought into an emerging market ETF.

I wanted to turn my discomfort with my vagina into something delectable, like the blogger who made sourdough with her vaginal yeast and served it to her Thanksgiving guests.

There was a particular kind of vagina makeup I read about that was only available in Scandinavia, which was appalling and also disappointing; I got on the waitlist. I never stopped meeting the challenge of being a vagina with a woman.

My vagina aspired to be the avant-garde—in the artistic sense: the pioneer, the innovator, yes, of course, but also in the military sense: the avant-garde stratégique, the force at the front engaging the enemy wherever he was found. In the presence of young women for whom a gesture might open new routes to power, I made a point of scratching my vagina in public. I knew other people had other sorts of practices—practices related to ending mass incarceration or eradicating factory farming, but as my guru said, know thyself. (My avant-garde vagina was, in the anarchist sense, sensational.)

I wore a T-shirt that said, WHAT'S YOUR VAGINA'S NAME? and as I walked down the street, women called out to me saying, "Venus!" "Isis!" "Madam President!"

With my phone, I took photographs of my vagina; they looked like extreme close-ups of Bryce Canyon.

When people asked me where I got my ideas from, I said my vagina. After reading Billy Collins's poem "Taking Off Emily Dickinson's Clothes" I spent the rest of the afternoon designing a button for my vagina that was both waterproof and comfortable and could be buttoned or unbuttoned with only my mind. I thought the way I said vagina, the frequency with which I peppered it into conversations, the tilt of my head when I said vagina, the tone of my voice when I said vagina . . . I thought it all might add up to something bigger than myself. Was my vagina here for the wrong reasons? Talking about my vagina made me feel better about myself, but not as good about myself as if I'd figured out a way to contribute something material to someone who needed it, like a house for an abused woman. I took some comfort in the fact that my vagina was local, organic, and ethically sourced.

My vagina had a ghost vagina, made up of everything that was moved aside to make room for it.

I google translated vagina, and it turned out that in Italian, Spanish, and Portuguese, it is still a vagina, though it is something else in Hebrew, something I couldn't say exactly, because, although I'd gone to Hebrew school and could read the Jewish script, Google Translate did not provide the little vowel markings beneath and beside the consonants, and when I tried to look up how to pronounce the vowel-less Hebrew word for vagina, a mechanical womanish voice came out of my computer saying over and over, vagina, vagina, vagina. Then I heard somewhere that in all languages, vowels are emotions and consonants are the intellect, and I wondered what a vagina without emotion might be like.

There was an empty space in my vagina where I had meant to put my accolades, and I worked hard to fill it with explanations and entertainments. I wrote a correction to my vagina the size of a story wherein I set right much of what, between the end and the beginning, I'd gotten wrong, starting with the fact that what I'd introduced my parents' guests to when I was five was not, in fact, my vagina but my vulva, which was a whole other story.

III.

It came to be that Simon, the son of a judge, was my third renter. I was turned to the wall so Simon could pretend to slip in through the window while, at his request, my vagina hid under the covers preparing to emerge as if from a coma, disoriented and grateful. In my Airbnb listing under AMENITIES, I'd included "humidified," "exterior lighting," and "self-cleaning," and as I lay there staring at the base-board, I wondered if I ought also to consider ticking "long-term renters welcome," to avoid the flexibility required in renting to different guests with different tastes.

A hand over my mouth and a dick in my hand and my vagina oozed into action. Simon's moves were alternately impersonal and embarrassing. At about the time he asked me to shut up and threatened to pull the knife he said was in the pocket of the jacket that he was still wearing, the door-bell rang. Once it became clear the doorbell ringer would rather ring and knock and walk around the perimeter of the property and ring and knock some more than leave, Simon got off me and told me to send the intruder away.

I opened the door to a broad-shouldered man who looked like an arborist I'd once dated. "I'm so sorry I'm late," said the arborist-look-alike, eyeing my bedsheet-for-a-robe.

I stood facing the threshold with Simon hiding behind the door.

The arborist-look-alike explained that he'd rented my vagina on Craigslist but had been unable to alert me to his late arrival, since after paying the rental fee, the email link on the listing had disappeared.

Just then, Simon began pressing something sharp against my sheeted rear. I told the arborist-look-alike that in fact, I'd never listed my vagina on Craigslist.

When the arborist-look-alike told me how much he'd paid the scammer in Florida, I felt bad but also, not responsible, and also a little bit insulted, since the Floridian scammer who'd copied my vagina's Airbnb listing had charged a third of my rate.

Still, the arborist-look-alike would not leave. I could feel Simon's impatience through the pressure of his concealed weapon, and I must have turned slightly, because all at once a great pain shot through the bursitis in my hip, and without thinking, I screamed and flung the door open, smacking Simon in the face, causing him to drop his weapon to cup his bloody nose with his hand. I grabbed the knife, which turned out to be not a knife, but a calligraphy pen. Simon promised to leave a "scathing" review, grabbed his shoes, and stormed off.

Then the arborist-look-alike pushed me back into the house saying he'd paid for my vagina and expected his stay. I stabbed him in the neck with the pen. After he bled out on my welcome mat, I dragged his body to the firepit, doused it in gasoline, lit it, and watched as a tree-shaped plume of smoke rose into the night and seeded the clouds. It began to rain.

THE AUDIO GUIDE

EDITOR'S NOTE: *Culp/ability. Such was the title of the museum audio guide received by this editor. As of publication, the museum intern who created the disquieting audio guide and sent its recording to the offices of this esteemed journal has yet to respond to our repeated inquiries. Every word of the audio guide is transcribed exactly as its creator recorded it, with the sole exception that the names of the museum director and the curator have been changed to protect the privacy of individuals. "Love is awful," the intern wrote in a note accompanying the audio file. Awful, this editor agrees, in the original definition of the word, as in: worthy of respect and fear.*

CULP/ABILITY
THE AUDIO GUIDE

[VOICE OF BELINDA HARKNESS, CURATOR:]
Welcome to the North Gallery Special Exhibit, *Culp/ability.*
On behalf of the museum, and its director, Leonard
Schmidt, it's a pleasure to have you with us. This is Belinda
Harkness, chief curator of modern and contemporary art
and your guide into the world of this special exhibition.

Culp/ability consists of six assemblages made over a
period of five years. During this time, the Artist—already
the youngest recipient of the prestigious Nevelson Prize
for Mythopoetic Art—was obsessed with a double murder
that took place in his hometown. The genesis of this collection dates back to the Artist's late twenties when the
crime was first reported and was still unsolved. It was
then that the Artist began a series of night-table sculptures based on his dreams. The sculptures, made of tissue and Vaseline, interrogated perspective by depicting
human body parts suspended with fishing line over min-
iature gates and windows. When, decades later, the crime
was solved, these sculptures became the inspiration for a
series of full-size assemblages. This series acts simultaneously as art and as provocation to a larger exploration of
guilt and responsibility.

[VOICE OF INTERN:]
I didn't take this internship because of you, Leonard,

though I'd seen your photograph— turtleneck and blazer— and knew your reputation. But since I've become a part of your world, my work has become a kind of homage: this mounting of exhibits for you to walk through; this editing of words that speak into your ears; this waiting daily for your call, which always comes. "Is Belinda there?" you ask. "Please hold . . ." I say, adding an inaudible "me" as I transfer your call.

[VOICE OF BELINDA HARKNESS, CURATOR:]
Shiver—

This object is filled with frantic energy. A large suit-case covered in dripping wax, pocked with postcards, and topped with a wind-tangled wig. Take a closer look. Can you see the postcard of the Icelandic Highlands signed by the Artist himself?

In 2001, the Artist visited Iceland on a Remote Art-ist Residency grant. There, while on a group tour of the fjords, a fellow tourist went missing. After rescue teams searched for hours with the help of the tour group partic-ipants, someone realized the missing woman had simply changed her clothes and gotten back on the bus unrecog-nized. She, too, had been helping in the search.

Notice, now, the shroud hanging on the wall behind the suitcase, as if anyone could take it off its hook and drape it over herself. Here the Artist invites the viewer to enter the locus of the missing, where the loss of self is visceral— sensual as well as methodical. The Artist's project is the

uncanny, conceived as what is both frightening and familiar. In an exhibition inspired by a killing, this assemblage
argues for homicide's shadow urge: to annihilate oneself.

[VOICE OF INTERN:]
As the song goes—*Ironic*. Unlike the song, however,
which is filled with non-examples of irony, the story
the Artist portrays is an actual example of the ironic—
because the woman who searched for herself couldn't
find her. You were right, Leonard. I was searching for
myself. Isn't every twenty-something who sleeps with her
boss's boss? And so were you, you said, when you found
me. Right here. In your place of work. How predictable,
your game of search and rescue. How many were there
before me? Long-haired brunettes with sunless skin and
expensive BFAs. Easy for you to say start fresh, start
again. A house, moist with damage, whose foundation is
rotten, cannot be built upon.

[VOICE OF BELINDA HARKNESS, CURATOR:]
Double Bed—
This bed was never meant to be slept on. One morning, the Artist awoke to news eerily close to home: a couple murdered in their sleep in the house not far from the
Artist's childhood address. The meticulously graffitied
headboard is covered in what appears to be runes or
possibly the key to a secret code and, as you can see, the
bright quilt is actually a great mass of loose red buttons.

This is perhaps one of the most disturbing pieces in the entire museum. Arrayed across two pillows are what appear to be human organs. And, look at the edge of the covers, near the center of the bed. A long, thin object projects from the pillow, a gore-covered ten-inch Henckels chef's knife. Here the Artist literalizes his dark inspiration. The couple was stabbed to death. The woman nine times. The man fifteen times. Face, neck, chest, arm, hand, heart, lung, esophagus, liver, pancreas, kidney, intestine.

When the museum first acquired the piece, after its transfer from the Artist's barn on his upstate property, the work was in a state of great disrepair. The human organs sculpted in wax and partially wrapped in gauze were deteriorating, and two full-time conservators were tasked with its restoration.

A decade ago, when the Artist, still relatively unknown outside of the alternative art scene, first displayed *Double Bed* at a downtown gallery, it caused a disturbance in the community.

"It's Not Sensationalism, It's Art," the *Voice* headlined, while its competitor, the *Observer*, led with, "Badly Made Bed." Thanks in part to this museum's championing of the Artist's oeuvre, *Double Bed* has since been recognized as one of the century's most influential works.

[VOICE OF INTERN:]
It's rumored that before the exhibit was put up, when the melted organs had been removed to the Department of

Conservation, the Artist and his lover used the bed for other purposes. That's something you might have suggested we do, Leonard. Back when I still resisted you. The more I held out, the more alluring I was to you. In that low voice of yours, you'd have told me you saw us nude on a buttoned bed, coupling in red, the outside world crackling and breaking beneath our marked skin. You used to speak to me in the heightened language of poetry.

[VOICE OF BELINDA HARKNESS, CURATOR:]
Bio Graphic—

This papyrus-draped embalming table with its four wheels shackled to the floor is one of the most visually arresting pieces in the exhibit. The murders that obsessed the Artist occurred in the killer's former childhood home. A schoolmate of the Artist was arrested for killing the couple whom he'd mistaken for his parents in a drunken stupor.

Part instruction manual, part warning label, the papyrus scroll is covered in comic strip panels depicting a man walking hand in hand into the afterlife with Anubis, Egyptian guide for the dead. Walk around the table and read the story as the Artist has painted it panel by panel. Anubis is depicted here as a young man in a blood-splattered leather jacket with the head of a jackal, his traditional red ribbon shown here as a tapeworm wound around his neck. Typically, Anubis is represented wielding a flail, his symbol a black-and-white oxhide hanging from a pole. In this version, however, Anubis crouches beside a headless skinned cat while holding out a Sobriety Circle and Triangle chip. By interpolating modern images where sacred symbols are expected, the story escapes simple interpretation. Instead, the Artist enacts a continuity between ancient cosmogony and contemporary trauma in the fractured images a survivor might use to express guilt.

Three-quarters of the way around, you'll reach the part where the man's heart is weighed against an ostrich feather to determine his eternal fate. In painstaking detail, the Artist paints a series of scenes in which the heart is shown as heavier than the feather, and a monstrous creature—zombie head, hippo body, baboon rear—approaches, springs, and then devours the man. A powerful rendering of our universal and deepest-held fears.

[VOICE OF INTERN:]
Aren't all hearts heavier than feathers, Leonard? And what of the afterlife you promised us? Wasn't I gladly devoured, bone by meaty bone, by you? "You're perfect—like a ballerina," you said as you wrapped your hands around my waist. Too late I understood it was the pas de bourrée you wanted, not the bloody, broken feet. Allow me to slip into some of your rich poetry: For you, I walked into the lake of fire. I held my bloody heart out to you, cupped your stubbled chin as you slurped its soup. I feel like Frida Kahlo, impaled by a trolley's metal, drinking tequila, and waiting for my bones to reset. Nothing left but to paint you attached to me by a red vein dripping into my lap.

[VOICE OF BELINDA HARKNESS, CURATOR:]

Repentance—

This assemblage began as a painting. The Artist had been working on a portrait of the killer and became so aggravated with it that he slashed it and hacked it. Only after dealing with it like it was a physical thing with skin did he get the idea of stuffing it with telephone wire and plastic bags so that it looked like its innards were coming out.

The finished work becomes, therefore, a product of the Artist's inquiry into the dark side of creativity. It is interesting to note that violent criminals and creative geniuses were once believed to share a set of "degenerate genes" leading to both mental illness and notable contributions to the arts.

The entire piece is covered in what appears to be grease-stained cling wrap and crowned with an old top hat, making it a truly three-dimensional specter. The alignment of the human form with recycled materials is a hallmark of the Artist's work.

[VOICE OF INTERN:]

I gave you everything you asked. My eyelids were hot with your breath. You said you wanted the world's dead lovers to feel our lovemaking and grieve. Tell me what to do now that you are done with me.

You once said life is a painting. Artists may change their minds, reposition a hand or remove an entire figure from a scene, but all paint eventually fades to reveal the true version hidden beneath. Did you mean I am your pentimento? Am I not good enough for you? Am I not finished enough? Am I still recording?

[Voice of Belinda Harkness, Curator:]
If Not Now When—

Meet the Artist: painter, sculptor, and disruptor. In this apparent self-portrait, the Artist is portrayed in his role as maker and destroyer. He holds in one hand, a paintbrush. In the other, a noose around the neck of a cadaver. The corpse is nestled at his feet. On closer look, the body looks like an older version of the Artist himself. Hanging from wires above the pair is a piñata of Dionysus, Greek god of wine and fertility and patron of the arts.

Although the killer's parents rallied around their son—posted bail and mounted his defense—the Artist's classmate was nonetheless sentenced to death. The crime, the trial, and the verdict all had a profound effect upon the Artist who felt a deep and wordless connection to both killer and killed.

[Voice of Intern:]
All this suffering. And for what? Would you post bail if I tried to kill you, Leonard? "Museum Intern, in Drunken Stupor, Stabs Airbnb Guests She Mistakes for Director and Wife." Would you finance my defense, though I'd knifed you in your bed? You say you are a moral man, so would you come to my aid? Remember the stenciled e. e.

cummings card you left on my desk after our first date: "love is more thicker than forget." You came back for it, saying you'd dropped it accidentally. Belinda smirked. Perhaps it was for your wife, but you made sure I thought it was for me. And so, I did. And I agree.

You always said I was too clever to be an intern, and I see everything now so clearly. The mistake everyone made—the police, Belinda, the Artist, even you and I—was in believing the killer, by stabbing the couple, was trying to kill his parents. Once a story ends, the clues are obvious. Drunk, he went back to his first house, not because he was confused about where his parents lived, but because he was going back in time. Because if he could kill his parents in the past, it would prevent them from ever making him. He went back to kill himself. It's hard to understand how I couldn't see this from the start.

I began this explanation what seems like hours ago, and yet the recording time says I've been speaking only minutes.

[VOICE OF BELINDA HARKNESS, CURATOR:]

My Detective—

We have here disordered objects presented in a kind of order: a set of handcuffs on a platter lined in squirrel fur placed on a tabletop between an optometrist's eye chart-cum-napkin and a carving knife. At the head of the place setting, a hand-shaped soap dish cupping a palmful of red wine. The quiet placement of this surreal mise-en-scène creates the feeling of a domestic moment captured unawares, and the title of the piece implies both danger and desire. The Artist's interest in Freudian psychoanalysis—specifically the concepts of life and death instincts: libido and aggression—is clearly on display. In society, our desires are repressed but may be accessed through artistic works via cathartic expression.

[VOICE OF INTERN:]
You were the everything that appeared before my eyes, and its perfect arrangement. You should know, Leonard, that I've altered *My Detective*. Now, on the platter lined in squirrel fur is a photo of me as a child, finger in my mouth, eyes closed. I drank the wine from the hand-shaped soap dish and replaced it with a clipping of my hair.

Why did I need the handcuffs, you may wonder? I'll allow Belinda, who recorded hours of commentary for me to edit, to explain—

[VOICE OF BELINDA HARKNESS, CURATOR:]
The handcuffs, a metaphor for taboo passion, both criminal and sexual, argue the ambiguity of our primal desires.

[VOICE OF INTERN:]
They were presented on such a soft, welcoming platter of temptation, Leonard. Like you, I could not resist.

INVENTED

I STAND ON THE sidewalk below an open second-story window and toss my apple core up and over the sill. A man comes to the window.

"What the hell?" he shouts.

(This is my husband before he is my husband.) He looks so alive; his cheeks are ruddy, and there's a bit of sweat on his brow that glistens in the sunlight, and looking at him makes me want to rumba. I giggle. Something bubbles up in me is what it is. Some excitement that the apple-core throwing through a stranger's window has released.

Then his face disappears, and his lovely leg presents

itself out the window. "I'm climbing down," he says. "Don't run away."

I hadn't thought to run away until he says not to, and so I consider it. Pro: Keep this ardent moment forever in my mind; con: Lose the chance to see if his torso is as sculpted as his leg is.

"My wife my life," he mumbles as he lowers himself out the window and drops to the ground at my feet.

This is the first sign that he is my invention.

Everything is made of mind. This is what all the awakened masters teach.

Also, his armpits. Our third date is a particularly humid day. We rent bicycles and ride out to the beach. We find a shady spot under some shrubs and begin to kiss. He licks the sweat off my upper lip; I pull off his T-shirt; wet rings make navy circles in the light blue fabric. I bury my nose in his long underarm hair, pull in a deep breath, and . . . no musk, no spice. No deodorant either. Just . . . nothing.

"This is not possible," I say, sitting up.

"Anything is possible," he says, pulling me on top of him.

About body odor: It helps with mate selection by indicating compatible or incompatible genes to avoid inbreeding. This could be why Ed has no smell: Were I able to sense his odor, I might be revolted and wish not to mate with him to avoid an incestuous relationship with my own invention. On the other hand, an invention is not a clone, and it may simply be that I've invented an odorless lover for myself so I can use my other senses to enjoy lovemaking while remaining clear of pheromonal influences that might weaken my resolve to remain childless. Then again, the whole unscented armpit thing might as easily be my own overzealous creativity, as I dislike most bodily smells, and Ed, tellingly, also has no bad breath, no sulfuric farts, and no foot funk.

In the argot of systems analysis (a language my ex spoke fluently), the unstable homeostatic system that was my life before Ed was colored by alternating states of dejected loneliness and fear of a lifetime of dejected loneliness. I'd broken up with my ex certain that I'd done the right thing—that despite his good looks and his good job and his good manners and his great apartment, he was not, nor would he ever be The One. I cried a lot, but I was proud of myself. My life pre-Ed, in other words, sucked a little.

To make it suck a little less, I enrolled in an online course called Lifeforce: Raising Your Personal Vibration, which offered a series of lectures and meditations for spiritual awakening. Though the promised sense of inner peace costs $399, 92 percent of the 1,818 learners claim the course exceeded their expectations. (As I was born Jewish, the number of learners seems doubly lucky.)

As a first anniversary gift, Ed pawns his watch so I can attend a weekend meditation retreat where I am further schooled in the projections that I have mistaken for my life. My apparent reality is *not* the way things truly are. What I perceive is only that—the reality that appears to me—and is no different from a dream.

The last night, I dream that Ed and I are desperate to have sex during a dharma talk and we keep trying secretly to do it, and the more we pull at one another's clothes and shift positions and try to stifle our moans and the more people notice or pretend not to notice, the hotter it gets.

When I walk in the door Sunday evening, I find my husband standing at the stove, stirring peanut butter into rice noodles. I notice his shoulders inside his shirt and feel immediately that they are meant to turn me on. I have just learned that I am habituated to reacting to the shape of his shoulders in this way. I cannot see his shoulders as joints connecting his neck and arms. I can only see my hands on his shoulders, my arms around his neck. . . . The process of projection happens so quickly that I almost don't notice it.

Nevertheless, I spin him around and kiss him hard. He tastes frighteningly perfect, and I am trying to be honest, so I tell him he isn't real.

"In ultimate reality," I say, "there is no such thing as inner or outer; past, present or future; you or yours." I bite his puckered lips.

"I agree," he says, taking off his pants. "There are no distinctions. Self and other merge." And we just barely remember to turn off the stove before flinging ourselves at one another on the kitchen floor.

This feels like recognizing a dream to be a dream while dreaming, and also recognizing that both in and out of the dream, you are about to come.

"I am deeply addicted and cling tightly to my projection," I say afterward as we eat the cold noodle dish from the pan.

Ed loves Matisse. Matisse is a love I can get behind. I can get behind an artist who paints the whites of a sailor's eyes green and then tells his patron the sailor was painted by the mailman. Invention after invention.

Ed has a postcard of *The Red Studio* that he keeps on his bedside table. We are lolling under the covers after sex when he reaches for it and begins to talk about it.

"Originally, the furniture was solid yellow, the floor was pink, and the walls were blue," he says.

It's what we all do, I think. Revise our world to fit the requirements of the moment.

He points to the yellow outlines of the table and chair, the patches of lighter red in the center, the blue line left where wall meets floor. "It's not laziness," he says. "He wants you to see he changed his mind."

I have changed my mind about my husband so many times (Ed is most beautiful when he sleeps; Ed is most beautiful awake. Ed is here to interrupt my loneliness; Ed is here to make me unafraid of loneliness . . .) that when I look at him, he's blurry. His edges won't hold. Even when he's sitting still, I think he's moving—a dark shadow above his knee, a different color on the wall behind one side of his head.

I notice that none of the artworks depicted in Matisse's painting has eyes or mouths.

"Would have been too much," Ed says. There's a crust of rheum in the corner of one of Ed's eyes, and when I turn so that I don't have to look at it, I notice the pile of half-eaten antacids on his dresser has grown exponentially. "He wanted his art to be an armchair for the weary."

Is this what I want from Ed? Is this why I am beginning to feel irritated with him? I raise my hand and place it flat over my invention's face.

"You're doing it again," he says, kissing my palm.

"What am I doing?"

"Mixing up art and life."

He's saying I'm wrong to believe everything I experience is of my own invention, but it's inarguable.

"Matisse agrees with me," I say.

"Oh?" Ed breathes next to me like an abstraction, both too close and too far away.

I point to the stools in *The Red Studio* that appear to support a plaster and a bronze, respectively. Each stool has only two legs. "Without the viewer supplying the missing legs, they're impossible."

"So, it's a collaboration," Ed says, putting the postcard back on the nightstand. "This," he says, wagging a finger between him and me. "Us," closing the distance between our bodies.

How can it be that he is here, except that I have conjured him? Day after day, I sit at the breakfast table opposite my new husband, close my eyes, and see nothing, only to open them and see him here. Again and again, every time I blink.

One day we visit an exhibit at the contemporary art museum. The featured artist, Mika Rottenberg, "considers how humans both comprise and manipulate matter." We spend an afternoon watching videos in which men and women in small rooms perform surreal tasks like sneezing out rodents or light bulbs or dishes of pasta.

"That was a little gross, wasn't it?" I say as we leave the museum.

Truth is, I can imagine a scenario in which I would be delighted to have a hamster sneezed from my husband. Or be so hungry that his sneezing me a plate of cacio e pepe would fill me with gratitude.

I watch Ed as he sits across from me in the subway car on the ride home, his head tilted, his eyes focused on the young mother next to him nursing her child, and suddenly I realize that *I* am the hamster-bulb-spaghetti sneezer. And he is waiting for me to feel the tickle, for my eyes to water, my nose to wrinkle, and, after some appropriate resistance, for me to produce some new, intact, and wholly disconcerting thing. He expects me, in other words, to furnish him with a little snot-product of his own.

That evening, I try casually to engage him in an

appreciation of how wonderful it is that we have only one another to care for.

"I always thought childless couples were a little sad," he says with a shrug.

From that afternoon on, living with Ed becomes awkward.

Ed narrates everything he does. I try a few different ways of asking him to shut up.

"Are you saying something I need to hear?" I ask from the other room.

He says no and continues to talk about *it's getting hot in here, where did I put that _____, I gotta change these shoes . . .*

"I can hear you!"

He says he's sorry. After a few minutes, he starts up again.

I decide he is the villager in that Zen story: All the monks are trying to meditate but the man from the village who's joined them keeps making noises—jostling in his seat, coughing, clearing his throat, plumping his medita-tion cushion. . . . Every day the villager's interruptions get worse—mumbling to himself, dropping things—until one of the monks can't take it any longer, turns, and glares at him. The villager understands immediately that his pres-ence is not wanted, so he gathers his belongings and pre-pares to leave. He is just outside the gate when the Zen master catches up to him, begging him to stay.

"I don't understand," says the man. "I thought I was a distraction."

"That is exactly why we need you," says the master, taking him by the arm and leading him back inside.

When my husband pisses me off, I call him, "Suchness."

In my latest Lifeforce lecture, I learn that while we imagine reality to be lacking, it is in fact, simply as it is: suchness. I call Ed "Suchness" to remind myself that what I call suffering and experience as suffering (his sleep-murdering snores; his climate change nonchalance; his habit of calling over a server and then holding them hostage as he deliberates what to order) is only illusion and misperception, and to reassure myself that enlightenment is not some far-off destination but has been here all along. I am already where I have always wanted to go.

Ed turns down another decently paid temp job. This time because the hours interfere with an open mic event that he has a particularly good feeling about. I take a deep breath to remind myself that the tightness in my chest and the sting in my eyes come not from Ed's inability to recognize my needs but from my confused belief that reality is difficult and painful.

"The Clever Lovers met their manager at The Room's open mic," he says. I swallow the urge to tell him he is acting like the opposite of a clever lover.

Instead, I say, "You are shrinking your already tiny fanbase, Suchness."

When I piss off my husband, he calls me, "Muchness."

We have our first actual argument. He comes home smelling like fast food and at first denies he stopped for a burger.

"You promised!" I scream.

"I am incapable of never eating an animal again," he says, a little sadly.

"You said you *love* animals."

"I do," he says. "I love animals so much I want to eat them."

"You are laughing at something I care deeply about," I say.

"I cannot live up to your standards."

"If it came to it, I think you'd eat *me*," I shout.

My husband stops then. He sits.

"I think you're right," he says.

I put down the knife I realize I am pointing at him.

"Under the right circumstances, with the right amount of hunger and desperation, having exhausted all other options, I do believe I might be capable of cannibalism if it were you," he says.

"What do you mean, *if it were me?*"

"Well, with your cleanses and organic vegan diet, I'd be pretty guaranteed, toxin-wise, a safe and probably quite wholesome meal." He looks up into my face. "In fact, now that I think about it, eating you would be a lot healthier than eating what I just ate at the Burger Shack."

And like that, Ed sets me into my animal body. I press

my lips against his greasy lips and slide my tongue over his meaty meat-eating tongue, and sit on his lap, my body melting like animal fat against his.

Makeup sex within a spiritual framework: Makeup sex is not forgiveness. I cannot forgive Ed, because even an invention has karma, and no one can erase someone else's karma from having done wrong. What I can do is prevent new bad karma from being created in the form of my own antagonism toward him. Makeup sex is an extension of lov-ingkindness. Making lov-ingkindess, I let go of my attach-ment to my disappointment in Ed.

Ed is not a robot. He has all the conditionality and unpre-dictability of a husband and is not programmed to satisfy my desires. It is not clear that a robot programmed to sat-isfy my desires would do so. In that, once my desires were satisfied, I might become dissatisfied. I don't mean that I'd have new desires—presumably, a well-programmed hus-band-robot would perceive or anticipate any new desires and move swiftly to satisfy them. I mean that I would become dissatisfied with having my desires satisfied. I think the robot programmers are already onto that. There are now sex robots programmed *not* to do as they are told. I think that's what I read. Or maybe they're programmed to not *always* do as they are told to appear less robotic, i.e., more human. In any event, I wonder what my relationship to a desire-satisfying husband would be. Boredom? Loss of interest? Is this why Ed does the stupid and annoying things he does?

I ask him if he has taken the banana out of the tennis bag that is crammed by the hot water heater in the closet.

"Yes," he says in that way that by now I should know means not *Yes, I removed the banana from the bag*, but *Yes, I wish to say what you wish me to say.*

A week later, we arrive at the tennis courts, and I reach into the pocket of the tennis bag and pull out my visor steeped in a sticky, brown banana roux.

SEVEN KINDS OF INVENTED HUSBANDS

1. The one who is so handy you don't need a plumber or electrician or vibrator
2. The one who loves his mother just the right amount
3. The one whose piss smells like the ocean and whose breath smells like the wind
4. The one who suffers silently, unobtrusively, when he's sick
5. The one who votes as if he has a womb
6. The one whose footsteps are light, voice is melodic, and words are precise
7. Mine

If my husband is a fiction, and if he causes me suffering, why not invent a way to get rid of him? Aside from the fact that delusion is the stirring necessary for awakening and that ridding myself of the delusion (Ed) would be ridding myself of my only hope for enlightenment, it's impossible. I cannot rid myself of my husband even if sometimes I may wish I could, because once an invention is set in motion, it cannot be uninvented.

It's not possible to uninvent the look on his face after the first time we made love when I told him I had a confession to make. That big-eyed stare, dazed and half-crushed, when he was certain I was about to tell him I was still with my ex. How that look transformed before my eyes as I told him instead that I had lied when I said I'd slept with plenty of men, and, in fact, he was only my second, third if you counted—which I didn't—a dildo I'd named Mr. President. His look of relief was such that I did not know whether I should kick him or kiss him.

It's impossible to uninvent the softness of the skin of his inner arm or the hardness of the muscle beneath it. The mole in the crease of his right eyelid. The sound of his voice, calling my name, the way in which my name in his mouth sounds like something needed. How do you uninvent the taste of a tongue that isn't yours but wants to be?

I could "kill my darling," but that would only make him my dead darling and his ghost would forever haunt me.

When I first tell Ed he's my invention—I've talked around it, but this time I actually say the words, "I invented you"— and that I'm not pleased with the creative production of my mind—he's just been fired from his fifth job in two years, and the rent is due—he does not take it well. I say it to be kind. After all, it's better than calling him irrevocable names which will only wing above us like evil faeries as I pretend to enjoy his mediocre cunnilingus during our now quite frequent makeup sex. Instead, I take responsibility for my objections to him.

He doesn't see it that way. He feels "emasculated."

Emasculated is an annoying claim. It literally means having both the penis *and* testes removed (as opposed to the removal of just the testes which is castration). My informing my husband that he is my invention is the opposite of removal; it is revelation.

He means, of course, that I've emasculated him metaphorically, which is even more annoying, since it means I've deprived him of characteristics traditionally associated with being a man, e.g., power, strength, independence . . . all of the qualities I wish he'd evince.

I take a deep breath and offer to go back to my teaching job which he encouraged me to quit so I could complete my thesis on the zuihitsu, a Japanese lyric essay of loosely connected fragments, literally "following the brush."

"Anything I say you'll hold against me," he says.

I tell him I am sorry, to which he insists, "I don't give a cabbage. It's sausage to me. It bothers me like a cardboard duck." Inadvertently providing further proof that he is the invention of his foreign-idiom-loving wife.

As I suspected, Ed wants a family. I want to figure out exactly what it is I'm supposed to learn from having him in my life so I can get to the next level of awakening. A child would be a huge distraction. I try to tell Ed this.

"You want spiritual growth?" Ed says. "Have a child. You want enlightenment? Have five!" He does not really want five. He'd settle for one. This means that I am not enough.

"This does not mean you are not enough," Ed tells me, stroking my hand. He wants immortality. My husband thinks he is nothing if he does not spread his seed.

"You tell me I am nothing anyway, so what does it matter if nothing procreates?"

We have arrived at the logic puzzle. If my husband is, indeed, a creation of my mind then what would our child be? A creation of my mind to the second degree? But no, the child would be half real. A crossbreed. Neither fiction nor nonfiction, a hybrid miscellany of illusory joys, temporary pains, strong opinions, and random magic.

In Old English, the companion word for *wife* was not *husband* but *wer*, pronounced /wɛr/, as in Where did I come up with you? Or, you wear me out.

I am supposed to be working on my thesis. Instead, I am typing my husband's name onto the screen of my computer in successively smaller font sizes. Ed Ed Ed Ed Ed Ed Ed Ed Ed Ed.

Until now, I have not created a problem that cannot be corrected by revision. At first, it works. With each smaller iteration, I gain a new measure of relief. It is good to watch what irks me diminish across a screen.

Then, "Honey!" Ed shouts from the other side of the door. I have told him not to disturb me when the door is closed, that my writing requires focus, and if he asks me when I'll be done or if I'm ready for dinner or anything at all really, it breaks my concentration and sets me back. "Done working, babe?" he says. "Almost ready for dinner?"

Alas, no invention is only what it is called. I am hungry and can smell the onions frying. Reality may be nameless and formless, but Ed and I seem to share both name *and* form.

"Coming," I say.

Over dinner Ed stares at me funny.

"Are you ovulating?" he says. "I think you're ovulating."

I tell myself at least I am clearer on the goal of transcendence. At least, after the months of meditation and study and deep relaxation techniques, I understand that what I experience as limited, solid, and confining, buddhas experience as spacious, open, and relaxed. At least there's that.

"You know I will never have your baby," I say to Ed.

If I didn't know I was dreaming, I might dream that Ed wants to have a child so badly he tells me one cold morning that if I'm sure I never want one, he'll have to leave me. If I didn't know I was dreaming, I might then experience great anxiety and grief. I might cry for days and drink lots of not-that-great wine and feel quite miserable all without realizing that Ed is only made of dream stuff. If I were only to realize I was dreaming, the image of living the rest of my life alone and unloved would have no more power over me than the image of a lovely man walking out a door.

One month after Ed leaves, in place of my claustrophobic imagination, I begin, at last, to experience the freedom of a new spaciousness. I walk around my neat apartment, eating what I like when I like. I watch the weather outside my windows change. I watch myself finish my thesis.

Then, Ed returns.

"Prove to me, logically, that I do not exist," he says, standing on the threshold.

"That's easy," I say, oddly relaxed. "Your body is not one thing but many. Toes, fingers, bone, blood." He steps inside. "And also carbon and hydrogen and oxygen." He takes off his coat and hangs it on the hook in the hall. "And also, electrons and neutrons and on and on until . . . you're emptiness. You are nothing."

"Sounds more like I'm everything," he says, walking into my arms.

Where precisely is this husband called Ed? Is he in those eyes, that belly button, those legs? I investigate each one in turn—spokes of hazel, specks of lint, splatters of freckles—and each proves to be but a collection of glimpses and tactile sensations held together by a concept.

He sits on the couch beside me, waiting.

I examine all the experiences that seem to make up my husband. Our brief and thrilling courtship, our small and lovely wedding, our house buying, our grocery shopping, our dinner sharing, our lovemaking, our fights. . . . The experiences I conceive of as Ed appear like dreams, and like a dream, they appear baseless and without support, unfixed, without root. It is all so tiring.

"You're even less real now than you were before," I say finally.

"And" he says, "have you similarly investigated yourself?"

So, I do. Lots of different glimpses: small feet, loose skirts, a reflection of a woman in a mirror, a headache, an injured wrist. Nothing that holds it all together.

"Have I invented you only to prove there is no real essence to myself?" I'm suddenly quite awake. "It seems I, too, am nothing more than an assumption." I feel a loosening.

Ed puts his hands on my shoulders, leans toward me, presses down.

"Who is it who says this?" I say, speaking into his mouth.

"Who is this who hears it?" he says, breathing into my ear.

JOKE, DECONSTRUCTED

1. THE JOKE

A WEEK BEFORE HIS wedding, the groom opens his front door to find his fiancée's sister. He invites her in. Inside the doorway, she smiles, opens her coat, and reveals her naked body. OMG, he thinks, my almost sister-in-law is offering to have sex with me! He pauses for a moment, unsure what to do—he's all out of condoms! Then he remembers: There's one stashed in the glove compartment of his car. He flings the door open and runs outside. There on the lawn are his soon-to-be in-laws, a crowd of them, clapping and cheering.

"You passed the test!" they say, slapping him on the back and congratulating him.

2. THE GROOM

Yes, I get a say. Surprised? Assumed I was just a prop in their little joke? A man who does what a man does—anything he can for a fuck? A man you laugh at or despise or pity or relate to, saying more about who you are than who I am?

Who *am* I? The guy who finally grows up and gets screwed for it.

After a couple years dating, Deb confesses: She doesn't want children—something about artists and mothers being mutually exclusive. If we marry, she says, I'll have to be okay with that. I get it, with a mom like hers, who'd want to be one? Still, makes you look at what you mean by marriage—exclusive ownership of another's genitals? Loving someone more than yourself? Family? Progeny?

When I first met Deb, it was like I saw myself for the first time in years. A drinker, a player, an operator, a bro . . . okay. But also . . . something else. Deb saw inside me. I can't say exactly what was there, and probably she can't either, but she saw it, and I saw her see it, and when she did, I felt it. Like when I was a kid, feeding my goldfish— the way their mouths opened and closed around the flakes I dropped, and the way it made me feel . . . I don't know,

good? Point being, with Deb, on our best days, I'm standing on a chair, feeding the fish again.

No problem, I tell myself. More money for us, more
sex on the dining room table, I think.

But it's actually harder than that. Right up until the
week before the wedding, I'm not sure, in my heart, that
I'm okay passing up descendants.

Then I see Nadine naked in front of me, and it's suddenly clear—I want out of the engagement. I want out
of this family with their moving targets and impossible
demands. I'm not okay with any of it. I want kids! Not with
Nadine, of course, because she's a piece of work. That's
why I run for the condom. I want my life back and my
future back and my future wants to go on and on with so
many kids, they'll be hanging from the rafters.

I'm too much of a wuss to tell Deb directly, though.
I hate disappointing her. When you disappoint Deb, the
disappointment doesn't stay hers; she has a way of giving
it back to you, multiplied. In other words, I don't want the
picture of what a failure I am to haunt me for the rest of
my days.

Fucking Nadine is my way out. Nadine will, of course,
tell her little sister, who will send me packing, not for
admitting that I value my legacy more than I value her, but
for being a typical asshole who can't say no to pussy, even
if it's his fiancée's sister's. Win-win!

Only it doesn't go that way. Instead, out there on the
lawn—clapping and cheering—are my almost in-laws,

congratulating and celebrating. What can I do? They circle tighter, applauding and toasting. I catch the eye of my almost father-in-law, and his smile says, there's no way out of this.

"It was never a question," I say. "Nadine is a beautiful woman." Did my almost mother-in-law smirk? "But Deborah is my abiding joy."

I don't see Deb until she steps out from a gaggle of cousins, beaming. She walks up to me and pulls me close. "You passed," she whispers. And I'm not sure if the look on her face—eyebrows raised, eyes popping—is delight or triumph, or both.

That night I can't get it up. I give Deb an orgasm anyway, but I'm too distracted and confused and what's more, I don't think she cares. She's glowing. But in a witchy way. How much does she know? I cannot ever ask, of course. And I cannot ever confess.

3. THE BIG SISTER

Shocked? Oh please.

Let me tell you about the first time I met Steven: It was a few months after he and Deb started dating, a week before she introduced him to the family, at the bar around the corner from my office where any number of partners typically end our week in a booth at the back. Four of us were competing in a game we call Worst-Case

Scenario—retelling our most awful cases as Shakespeare scenes. I was well on my way to winning Madam Bard for the week, when a man slid off a barstool, walked to our table, and said to me, "Excuse me, but you look so familiar."

An ex once told me I looked like the "after" photo to my sister's "before."

So, this was Even Steven, I thought. Deb's previous boyfriend, (Moody) Rudy was a musician who'd outmatched even her changeability. I guess I wore Deb down with my arguments for finding someone more stable, because after a year of Sturm und Drang, Rudy was finally out, and Steven was in.

Why didn't I tell Steven who I was? Because I wanted to see who *he* was. Yes, my little sister is the "before" me. When the ex said it, he meant in the beauty-makeover way. When I say it, I mean in the hurtable way. Deb's an artist; her vulnerability is her canvas.

Beautiful girls like me have to be fierce to be seen, and I have always been competitive. I distrust men and I have a steady, unfulfillable need for men. You want the Freudian interpretation? Doug's not my real father. How did I know? It wasn't hard for a night-owl kid in a thin-walled house with a mother who nightly railed against her lousy Good Samaritan husband to figure it out. No one but Doug knows I know.

Steven flirted. I observed, which he interpreted as an invitation to flirt more. He was a decent flirt, i.e., he had

the goods: charm, looks. But something was missing. A
specificity to his attention. He was like a dart in search of
a target. I got up to use the restroom. When I returned,
Steven was back at the bar, seated next to a woman with
red hair. She was what I will be in fifteen years. Alluring
and alone. I will choose alone like Coco Chanel did—like
a posh accessory. I watched them from my seat. It was
like watching a movie you'd never seen but could perfectly
predict. They left together.

Growing up, Deb and I fought and made up constantly. It
was always over something trivial: a misused hair dryer, a
tripped-over sneaker. Once we did not speak for a week. It
was the summer after my freshman year of college. Deb
asked me to find out if a guy she liked liked her. My investigation resulted in his asking me out.

"You're incapable of doing anything for anyone else,"
she said.

I know exactly what I am and am not capable of. Deb,
on the other hand, had no idea what she was capable of.
Specifically, whether she was capable of loving a liar and
a cheat. That's why I seduced her fiancé the week before
her wedding.

My plan? We'd fuck; I'd slip into Steve's sweats, go out
on the lawn, and present my case: As soon as he'd seen I
was naked, Steve ran into his bedroom to get me clothes,
then sat me down for a heart-to-heart about family and
fear, or love and honor, or maybe my habit of proving my

worth by proving the unworthiness of everyone else. . . . Some such compelling case. I can convince a jury of whatever I want. Then I'd tell Deb the truth and let her decide.

Turns out it was easier than that after all.

"Wait one minute," Steve said, before rushing out the door, "I'll be right back."

4. THE MOTHER

Of course, I figured he'd fail. He already had.

A couple of months ago, I asked Deborah to bring over a jacket she'd borrowed for some opening. I stepped out of the shower, and the doorbell rang. Usually the girls just walked in, but she must have forgotten her key. When I opened the door, there was Steven, my jacket slung over his arm. In that moment, I realized what I'd really wanted wasn't my jacket back but my daughter. I hadn't seen Deborah in weeks—between her side gigs and social life, she'd all but forgotten me, and now she'd sent her boyfriend instead of coming herself. A familiar heat rose in my gut— part anger, part dare.

"Well, this is a surprise," I said, pulling my shoulders back and placing my hands on my hips. I could feel the silk flaps of my robe pull open, and Steve's eyes slip down the naked length of me.

It's a form of hypochondriasis, only instead of thinking the pain is cancer, you think it's arousal. So, you go to a man to prove you're right, hoping all along he'll convince you you'll heal yourself in time.

I stepped toward him, pretending not to notice that the robe was open, and at the last moment, took the jacket from his arm, thanked him, and turned away. What did I expect? He'd clear his throat and say, "Oh, Ruth, it seems your robe is slipping open. I'll just toss this jacket to you so you can cover up"? It's not my fault I can still get any man. But it *is* his fault that he was about to go for it.

Men are children; women are girls who've figured that out. My girls: Nadine and Deborah. Born a year apart and different as N and D. Nadine: tall, fast, wanting to be an astronaut when she grew up. Deborah: watchful, sensitive, insisting for a year that she was a cat. Now Nadine is a member of the bar and a perfectionist. Now Deborah teaches barre and is a performance artist.

What Deborah calls art I call embarrassment. She says that's my way of not owning my truth. If by truth, she means my vagina, I tell her I own mine, I just don't sit mine on a museum floor in front of a world-famous painting and open it up for strangers to see. *Reenacting the Portrait* got her an indecent exposure violation; her sister got her a fine reduction.

"My desire is not your object," Deborah wrote in her artist's statement. "It is my subject."

What I've brewed from the subject of my desire could be distilled and drunk for years, but no one cares to give a mother and thirty-year wife a license to sell that kind of liquor. I do understand Deborah's need to shock; when you're not beautiful, you have to find other ways to get attention. When I was young and not beautiful, I did the same. Only what shocked in those days was stealing things you could afford and getting knocked up by a perfect stranger. Every woman has her own tragedy, and mine is that I was unable to shock. Doug convinced the store owners that my petty larcenies were honest mistakes, married me before I began to show, and moved me out here for a fresh start.

When the girls were in middle school, a family with three children moved in across the street. The first time we met the new neighbors, the man and kids were emptying boxes from the car; the woman was inside. I shook the man's hand and introduced my girls.

"These are my sons," he said, naming each. "And this is my adopted daughter."

"That was fucked up," Nadine said that night at dinner. At eleven she was already an expert at prosecuting offenses. "Either she's his daughter or she's not."

She looked pointedly at Doug. He reddened. She got up from the table, and he went after her. I don't know what they said to one another but from that day on, it was Doug and Nadine. Textbook irony: Deborah and I have never had that kind of bond.

I stood outside with the rest of them, clapping till my hands stung. I know the look of a man who wants what he can't have, and I know the look of a man who thinks he's about to get it. The first was Steve in my doorway; the second was Steve in his. At least Deborah thought he'd passed.

5. THE FATHER

Deborah came to me about a month before Steven proposed.

"We're going to marry," she said, "but before you walk me down the aisle, I need you to do something for me." I was supposed to get Nadine to test Steven. Was it one of her *happenings*? "No, insurance," she said.

"Someday your mom and I will be gone, and all you'll have is your sister." I didn't want her to blame Nadine.

"I won't," she promised. "I'll blame him."

Maybe there was a part of me that wanted him to fail. I thought Deborah could do better. I didn't think Nadine would mind being right about Steven. She'd come to me earlier saying I should break them up. I told her I wasn't that kind of father. "What kind of father are you?" she asked. That hurt.

"Make her think she thought of it," Deborah said.

I told Deborah she was tempting fate.

"I never understood that expression," she said. "Fate is fated. What's there to tempt?" She was an artist; she could make things make sense that never should.

I put the idea into Nadine's head, but Deborah put the idea into mine.

I love my daughters, but I don't understand them. My wife was another surprise. I thought Ruth would hate the idea. She always said Deborah trusted the wrong people. Instead, she endorsed it. Was she still rooting for Deborah's ex? When Deborah told us about Rudy's ups and downs: "He's a keeper," said Ruth. Deborah had been annoyed, thinking her mom was being sarcastic. Only I knew she meant it. I saved Ruth from a life of terrible ups and downs, and she will never forgive me for it.

In the end, he ran out like he couldn't get away from Nadine fast enough. It must have hurt Nadine's pride that the one man she couldn't seduce would be her sister's husband. His racing out was only half the shock though.

Steven face-to-face with me on the lawn brought me right back to the last time I saw my brother. Just after he told me he'd knocked a girl up.

"It was never a question," Steven said.

I was shaken.

It was exactly what my brother had said when I asked why he hadn't offered to marry Ruth.

6. THE BRIDE

It was easy.

Steve was horny. My last period had me in bed for days with terrible cramps, and then I was too preoccupied with the wedding to focus, so we hadn't fucked in a month. I promised we'd do it after the rehearsal dinner.

"*Right* after. Put this in the glove compartment," I said, handing him a single ribbed condom. Then I made a show of throwing out his Trojan 100-pack, saying they'd expired.

I gathered the extended family outside his place to witness his running out for the condom. And of course, he did.

Then, "Woohoo!" I started clapping and cheering and everyone joined in. The applause, the kudos, the esteem: Steven the hero! Steven the Übermensch!

They think they know me. They think I'm the flighty artist unable to take care of herself. The one who needs to be protected—from herself and from the world. But they were in *my* performance piece. Typecast and playing their parts—horny groom, sexy sister, unloved mother, feckless father. I was the deus ex machina.

Why did I do it? For an income, a beard, and power.

An artist needs a patron. Steve's a solid wage-earner and a decent fuck. Boring compared to Rudy, yes, but someone you can count on for orgasms and rent. Problem was, he'd eventually want out—whether for variety or for kids. Solution? Find a way he's guaranteed to stay.

Here's a little lesson in personality: There are people who don't care about what anyone thinks of them, like Nadine. And there are people who care about nothing more. That's

Steven. Deep down he's ashamed of his shit morals. I have always had a superpower. With a look, I can make you feel like you're the most authentically beautiful being on this planet, and like a cloud across the sun, I can sweep that all away, leaving you a shivering miserable putz.

I won't go into his childhood trauma, but let it be understood that the need I saw in Steve was deep. I understand the lengths a person will go to be known as they require.

Sew your mouth shut and sit outside a supreme court building and you will be heard. Bury yourself up to your nose in soiled diapers and you will be seen.

Everything is a choice. In a patriarchy, a woman can be a great artist or a good mother. I chose art. Steve's choice, old as time: In the face of temptation, was he weak or was he strong? Men convince themselves of their power all the time. Then they perform it.

I saved him from public humiliation, and this is the happy ever after. Every couple makes their own marriage pact. In ours he suspects he's just another dick, but I treat him like he's not, and in exchange for his sticking around, he greets his longed-for self in my eyes.

Steve suggests we get dinner at The Roadhouse where that red-headed waitress gives him extra hot sauce and rubs her hand over his when she gives him the check. "Sure," I say. It's just another item charged with debt in the ledger of our arrangement. I won't say whose cake is had or who's eating it, but I will tell you, it's rich.

ᗪEING STEVIE

SEE THE STAGE. THE short woman in the platform shoes is me, as Stevie Nicks. The obese woman in the third row is Maeve, my mother. She's next to Walter, my father, the handsome man overdressed in a jacket and tie. My mother would never admit it, but she doesn't want to be here. She doesn't like seeing me on stage—higher than her, louder than Walter, the center of everyone's attention. Walter is King and Maeve is Queen, and if the Princess gets too big, then the whole thing falls apart.

Walter is uncomfortable: Maeve's ass is over her seat and pressing into the side of his leg. He is holding her hand and trying to watch the drummer, trying to be one with the drum set, not with the woman in the filmy dress who it's too easy to forget is his daughter.

What I Remember of My Childhood

- When I was eight, I spent a night sleeping outside and awoke understanding that a raindrop is a tree is a boulder is a bird . . .
- When I was twelve, I realized my body was not only my trap but also my trap door.
- When I was fifteen, I fell in love with a young magician. All summer long he brought birds back to life, levitated coins, juggled disappearing knives. In the end he left for France and never came back, and I mowed and mowed my parents' lawn. Each day I mowed; each night the grass grew back, thick with secret, lying things.

There's a reason for costumes. My body is unremarkable—slim, boyish, utilitarian. Separately, my body parts are perfectly satisfactory, but together the impression they create is no more than a physical marker of a person. My body is a placeholder for a self. Enter Stevie.

The point is, the reason I do this—make my living performing as a '70s icon while my fellow classmates (Yale '13) are busy being anesthesiologists and bankers—is to not be me, little *m*. My shrink, Dr. Gay, agrees, says the point is to be Me, big *M*, but he wants me to do it as Myself.

That's not likely to happen anytime soon. There's a town in China that makes a third of the socks that exist on the planet. Being Stevie is like being that town. *Stand back. Stand back.*

<u>What Being Stevie Gives Me</u>
- A deeper voice.
- Songs like exorcisms.
- Plumed velvet, crystal beads.
- Mystery in place of nothingness.
- The illusion that illusion is enough.
- An audience like a giant sea anemone waving back at me.

The incredibly good-looking guy in the front row with the ridiculous grin on his face is my boyfriend, Brian. He doesn't care about Stevie. He wants me. He's wanted me since college when we were in the same Mandarin class and I convinced the teacher it was unethical to give a test on Rosh Hashanah. He wooed me by explaining that heart cells isolated on Petri dishes bounce to their own rhythms, but heart cells placed beside one another organize themselves into a collective beat.

Brian's figured out that if he stares into my eyes, he'll see only me. When I sing with my eyes closed, he closes his eyes too. When I look out into the blast of light that obliterates the audience, he stares into my eyes and what he sees is his personal guardian angel. The one who will save him. Brian needs saving like the rest of us, but with Brian, you feel how much he needs saving. If you're paying attention. If you're not, then what you feel is inferior. It's induced. I know this because Dr. Gay has explained induced feelings to me: Induced feelings are the ones you feel that are actually someone else's projected into you.

Brian's insecure, so when you're with him, he makes you feel insecure. Over dinner with friends, he'll mention a big case he's trying the next morning and someone will say, "In bocca al lupo!" proud she knows the Italian for good luck—literally, in the mouth of the wolf—and he'll respond, "Crepi il lupo!" which no one will understand but which Brian will explain means "May the wolf drop dead," and everyone will think, okay, that's interesting, but then he'll throw in a little lesson about the origin of the expression: Traditionally, when a hunter killed a wolf in the Apennine Mountains, he went door-to-door in his village carrying the wolf skin as a bag into which villagers dropped presents in gratitude for his saving their livestock, making the luparo a truly lucky guy, which will cause everyone else at the table to feel stupid and uninteresting.

Not me, though. I know it's his insecurity I feel, so when I'm with Brian I feel like the most together chick around. I feel my vision is 20/10—what you can only see at ten feet away, I can see at twenty. Dr. Gay says I'm with Brian because I'm working out my daddy stuff.

"No, that's why I'm with you," I correct him, and he smiles. When I get something right, he likes it. It turns him on. I want to turn on Dr. Gay. I want Dr. Gay to get down on his knees one Thursday morning at 10:15 and beg me for it. That's what I'm thinking about when I'm singing. That's what's making Brian smile and Walter sweat and Maeve want to look away.

Where I Would Be If I Weren't Stevie
- Married, with kids in the suburbs.
- In my kitchen, dehydrating kale leaves.
- In the yard, picking ticks off the dog.
- In the carriage house, on top of the UPS man.
- On the phone with my kid's teacher explaining why my daughter hides every time it's her turn to share.

Without Stevie, I'm afraid of everything: crowded places, sudden aneurysms, that I'm no better than anyone else. Anything goes wrong—another rogue state develops nuclear capabilities, I accidentally pee when I sneeze, Monsanto corners another sector of our food supply, another hundred thousand acres burn—the first thing I think is that my days as Stevie are numbered. Not that my days are numbered. My days as Stevie are numbered. When I'm Stevie, time disappears. As does my slight lateral lisp, the need for sarcasm, and my certainty that I'm loved for the wrong reasons.

Walter and Maeve see Stevie as a phase. They're waiting for me to apply to graduate school and make Brian their son-in-law. "This is my life," I say. We are all impersonating something: The male sea horse gets pregnant and gives birth; single Japanese women rent husbands by the hour to solve problems with their neighbors. Even Stevie takes off Stevie before she goes to bed.

Dr. Gay says I don't want to look at myself and that's why I turn myself into Stevie. I tell him, maybe, but maybe that's not so bad: Maupassant ate lunch at the Eiffel Tower because it was the only place in Paris from which he could not see the Eiffel Tower.

Dr. Gay says it's not healthy to take being someone else so seriously. I tell him maybe, but the Portuguese poet Fernando Pessoa created more than seventy heteronyms—each with a different writing style, education, and political view—and two of them are considered among the most influential Portuguese writers of all time.

Dr. Gay says, "But you are not embodying a heteronym, you are impersonating someone who already exists." To which I say, "Maybe, but she is now in her seventies and I am being her when she was twenty-nine, which you could say is an invention, which you could say is a creation, which you could say is embodying a fictional character out of time." To which he says, "Time's up."

I hate it when I have to sing the last song. *And is it over now, do you know how? Pick up the pieces and go home.* But I'm an artist, so I love to hate the last song. I love it so much I sing it like I've never sung it before. I sing it like it's the last song I'm ever going to sing: starting low, squatting at the mic, layers of my dress in waves around me, my eyes closed, the song too big for me, tearing at me, and soon I'm possessed—shoulders rising, head back, spinning. I'm a dark liquid, spotlit and steaming. I'm wrapping myself in my scarves, lifting my arms like wings, swelling, calling, disappearing, and reappearing. My voice comes up from the center of the earth, through the floor, through my groin and guts and ribs, and then my heels hit the stage again and again, and I'm a green light never going to turn red, and the audience goes wild.

<u>Secrets of Singing as Stevie</u>
- Sing as if you're just about to lose everything.
- Sing as if your personal ethical code is approaching its "use by" date.
- Sing as if your future is winking at you from just outside the exit door.

We all have the means of our own escape. It's based on our level of creativity, our level of desperation. Take, for instance, Henry Box Brown: Born enslaved in Virginia in 1815, at age thirty-five he shipped himself in a box marked DRY GOODS—three feet long by two feet wide—via railroad, steamboat, ferry, and delivery wagon from Richmond to the Philadelphia Anti-Slavery Society, where he emerged from the box singing.

I cheated on Brian with Josiah, an old high school crush. It made me feel good for about as long as the afterglow of the orgasm, which seemed like enough at the time. Josiah is short and smooth—a championship runner with legs tight as twine. I was leaving a meeting with my manager when I bumped into him in midtown after not having seen him in a decade. We got lunch and then went back to his place. Clichéd and ridiculous, except for his tongue, which was long and pointy and reminded me of a lizard's.

Brian and I aren't married. We never will be. Still, when I see him here, standing and clapping and whistling for an encore with the rest of them (I can see the audience from where I wait stage right for the perfect pitch of desire before stepping back onstage for one more song), I'm frightened he'll figure it out. I'm afraid he'll see it on me somehow—my infidelity, my betrayal—and then I'm angry that I'm fearful, because who is he to make me feel this way? And my heart races and my pulse quickens and just like that, I'm more attracted to Brian than ever.

Brian mouths, "I love you" as I step once more into the lights.

I told Dr. Gay I cheated on Brian because I could feel his seriousness breathing down my neck. I also told him I discovered via the internet that in Hawaiian there's no word for adultery—the closest term translates as "mischievous mating." Plus, if I had been one of the kids in the Stanford marshmallow experiment, I would not have resisted eating the first marshmallow long enough to get the second.

This, I argued, is not so much a result of a lack of self-control as a disbelief in the promise of a delayed reward.

Dr. Gay thinks I cheated on Brian because I secretly want to get caught and I need proof of my innate badness. Plus, Dr. Gay noted that Josiah is, like himself, short and knows about my childhood and runs. Dr. Gay says I have unresolved Oedipal issues; I have read Sophocles and still have little idea what this actually means, though Dr. Gay says it often as if he believes—the way some people believe in speaking louder to a foreigner—eventually, I will understand.

After the show, my parents and Brian come backstage to see me. Each plays their part: Brian won't take his arm off my shoulders, so everyone knows I'm his; I don't love it, but I get it. Walter is talking to everyone he can, letting them know that I'm his daughter and that I get my rhythm from him. He talks up the drummer, who thinks Walter's talking about his CD of Glee, not Grieg, and who's laughing and thinking my dad's a pretty humorous guy while my dad sprays his charm like a dog marking everyone around him. Meanwhile, Maeve is working at being likable. She's learning everyone's name, smiling, complimenting the lighting designer, the sound technicians, the stagehands, so no one feels small. Maeve is a small woman in a big body. The smaller she feels, the bigger she gets. The bigger she gets, the smaller she feels.

I drink too much at the after-party. Brian says he doesn't mind that I drink sometimes, but back at my apartment, he doesn't want to kiss me. I offer to go down on him, but he doesn't want it. The only guy I ever heard of who doesn't.

.   Sometimes Brian talks wistfully about our 2.1 kids and our white picket fence, but he knows we do not see the same world. Take our recent discussion of the rare disorder, apotemnophilia, whose victims are obsessed with wanting their own healthy limbs amputated. They're so desperate, they'll try to do it themselves: lie on a railroad track, use their own saw. A Scottish surgeon who successfully performed two such healthy limb amputations was scheduled to perform more when the story broke and his hospital forced him to stop. Brian quoted the Hippocratic oath to do no harm. I said, "If it makes them feel better, isn't that a cure?"

Instead of fooling around, we fall asleep watching old episodes of *Saturday Night Live*. Tina Fey and Jimmy Fallon sing us weird lullabies through the night.

I have what I call My Seesaw Theory of Love: Balance is impossible. Someone's always rising; someone's always falling. Someone's always just about to get the bird's-eye view of the sunburn on someone else's scalp.

<u>On the Bottom of the Seesaw, Heavy with Love</u>

- I'm prone to catastrophizing, which Dr. Gay says is a sign of a weak ego and is linked to early death—to which I tell him it sounds like he's catastrophizing.
- I'm all arms and fingers, groping during sex; I

hold Brian so close he can barely move. I don't so much kiss him as chew on him.

* I'm immune to compliments.

<u>On the Top of the Love Seesaw</u>
* I can't stand Brian's smells: his pillowcase, his aftershave, his hair.
* I can tell by a look what anyone needs from me.
* I can lead an audience wherever I want.

It's a bad idea to wake up with Stevie still on. In the movies when the leading lady wakes up with makeup on it's perfect: sultry mascara smudge; puffy, kissable, lipstick-smeared lips. I look like shit. I'm still wearing the wig—the one from *Rumours*, long, blonde, and straight—only it's matted from my sleeping in it, the bangs are creased, and there's a bird's nest at the nape of my neck.

"Coffee?" Brian is seated at the end of my bed, steaming mug in hand. His eagerness annoys me. He leans in for a kiss.

"My breath," I mumble, taking the coffee and offering my cheek. I drink, and Brian sits there watching me, a weird expression on his face.

"What?" I say, but he just sits there watching me like he's secretly got nipple clamps on and someone's pulling at the chain.

I pull off the wig and begin fishing along my sweaty scalp for the sixteen hairpins that have held my own hair down for the last seventeen hours, all the while sucking at the coffee like it's the only thing that can save the morning. Something hits my lip as I drain the mug, and at first, I think it's a piece of glass. Quickly, I put the mug down and bring my hand to my mouth to see if I'm bleeding. Brian lifts his eyebrows beginning to smile, as if he knew the piece of glass was there all along.

"What the fuck?" I say, and his eyebrows fall, his face darkens. Suddenly, I realize it's not a piece of glass. I stick two fingers into the mug, and one slips right into the ring.

"Oh no," I say, and Brian's face brightens.

My first thought: Stevie doesn't wear a ring. My second thought: I could have swallowed this and bled to death internally. My third thought: I'd never wear a ring this big. My last thought before Brian interrupts my thoughts: This is what Dr. Gay would call a pivotal moment.

According to Dr. Gay, pivotal moments are opportunities that sit like perfect discs on the floor of your life. By stepping onto one and shifting your weight just slightly you can pivot on the spot and see something that just a moment before you couldn't.

What I see now is Mae Rose Owens, the woman I read about in an article about sinkholes in Florida, watching as a sycamore in her yard is pulled downward by the roots with a swish and a shloop as it disappears. Eventually, the opening grows to more than a hundred feet deep and three times as wide and swallows cars, the town pool, her house.

<u>Where I Was When I First Heard Stevie's Voice</u>
- Gymnastics camp, age fourteen, "Dreams" from a counselor's boom box, loneliness liquefied in a voice. Chest-thumping truth-telling, nostalgia for what I had not yet lost. Voice the sound of a train leaving, and over and over again, *You will know*.

When I give back the ring, Brian says, "If you don't want to marry me, then I guess that's it." I say I guess so. He looks as if he might cry.

Stevie doesn't cry—she makes you cry. That's her genius. She's blonde-banged and full-lipped, and you could cry just looking at her.

The next week I'm on my way to see Dr. Gay and there's a mime in the subway station. He's wearing all black except for white gloves and a white plastic mask over his black hood—half Mardi Gras, half *The Seventh Seal*. I watch as he does the trapped-behind-a-wall bit, escapes through a window, is caught in a cage, pulls himself along an invisible rope, moonwalks, stands on his elbows, twirls on his head. Now he's a taxi driver nodding into his mobile, now a straphanger airing his armpit. He's on an elevator; he's walking in wind; he's a wind-up toy; he's a marionette. Easy listening for the eyes—he's double-jointed and can roll his torso like a giant marble around his spine.

I feel the wind of an approaching train, as the mime falls into a steep backbend, nearly touching his head to the platform behind him, then back handsprings to his feet just as the train pulls into the station. That's when I notice his collection hat on the ground has a cardboard sign in it saying REMEMBER ME. A couple of people drop coins in the hat. One woman gives him a bill, and he mimes kissing her feet.

As I step onto the train I think, everyone's eventually forgotten. Some more eventually than others.

FEEL BETTER

I WENT TO THE doctor because I felt too much. Ever since puberty I had, but upon turning thirty, it had become insufferable. My fingers throbbed, the bottoms of my feet itched, the skin behind my knees prickled, my nipples stung, my hair stood on end, and I couldn't sleep for all the feelings that burned through me.

The first doctor had me lift my knees then lift my elbows into his downward-pressing palms.

"Lovely *and* strong," he said to my husband.

This was supposed to make me feel better. Or maybe to make my husband feel better, since that's who he was

talking to. I did not know if lovely women received better or worse healthcare than unlovely women, but I'd
read a study that concluded women in general received
inferior medical care compared to men. Furthermore,
the study showed women accompanied by men received
slightly better treatment than unaccompanied women or
women accompanied by another woman. This was why I'd
brought my husband. Not to have the two of them appre-
ciate my loveliness.

The second doctor told me to stop crying and pull
myself together. This too was supposed to make me feel
better. To set me straight onto the path of recovery. Which,
in a way, it did: I stopped crying because it was hard to cry
when I was mad. Possibly the second doctor had decided
to employ some psychological trickery to help his patient
move away from self-pity toward rehabilitation, in which
case he was a martyr, willing as he was, to step directly
into the path of an über sensitive woman's anger in order
to secure the forward momentum of her improvement.
The aforementioned anger might have been why the second doctor referred me to the third doctor.

The third doctor was an expert who favored the royal
we: "We do not know much about your condition; we are
going to keep working on your case; we will not rest until
we have gotten to the bottom of your situation."

This was a wonderful way of telling me he was not
going to help me such that I felt I still owed him thanks.
And money of course, which is the currency of gratitude.

Also, the currency of desperation. I spent a great deal of money on my over-feeling body which required X-rays, blood tests, CT scans, MRIs, even a spinal tap. After that, my still very much, if not more, over-feeling body required experimental (read, more expensive) medications to be swallowed, injected, inserted, and applied.

The fourth doctor was a shrink. "Didn't you grow up in a family that didn't feel *anything*"? he said. When he said that, I felt a disconcerting extra heartbeat that I felt the urge to cough away. It was unsettling enough to feel this skipping, flip-flopping flutter in my chest as I sat still on his couch, but then I felt something altogether new—I felt what the shrink felt. Boredom. The shrink's boredom was shocking. Not because I'd bored a shrink—I'd expected that from the start, but because I felt his boredom. In me. And yet I knew it was the shrink's boredom. The shrink's boredom appeared in a space in my lower back like an ache, but with a certain unfamiliar signature that I recognized immediately as the shrink's.

"I feel that," I said.

The shrink just sat there.

I did not return.

Other than over-feeling physical sensations and once feeling the boredom of a shrink, nothing seemed to be wrong with me. But I wasn't getting better. "Try mindfulness," suggested my husband, who always felt better when making suggestions.

I tried. I felt my lungs fill and empty and fill and empty, which was an actionable meditation technique. But it was also distracting when I was supposed to be doing something like making a sandwich, because if I was noticing each in-breath, then I wasn't noticing that I was spreading the almond butter not on the bread but on the cutting board, which caused a fight with my husband who already thought I spent too much money on almond butter, which he also thought was an unconscionable source of protein since almonds required an inordinate amount of water which was desperately scarce where they were grown in California, and he neither agreed that California required my buying its almond butter to support an economy that represented a crucial fifty-five electoral votes, nor did he understand that almond butter needed to be raw and organic to be truly healthful which cost even more, and "Now look at all this waste!" he said.

"You try spreading nut butter on bread while feeling the grain of the hardwood floor through your socks and the seams of your stretch pants running up the insides of your thighs and the skid of soap residue on the knife handle," I said. "Not to mention *your* resentment and impatience and guilt and remorse," which stunned us both—my condition was worsening! This shut him up for a bit since it named not only his feelings but also my worsening problem which he could not solve, though he spent nights on a symptom checker looking up Hypersensitivity: Causes, Possible Conditions, What to Do . . .

I felt the blob of badly almond-buttered bread scrape its way down the eight inches of mucosa lining my esophagus and into my stomach, which I felt spraying its acid and churning the mess before sending the paste into my small intestine, which I felt squiggle and bulge until the unabsorbed slop entered my large intestine, which I felt pushing the mass into my rectum, which, yes, I felt as it accepted the shit that was technically not yet shit because I had not yet shat. Was mindfulness really all that?

I felt my clitoris. A lot. Orgasm was the only way to turn off the other feelings. It felt like the hand of God. Okay, maybe it felt like the hand of my neighbor who gardened shirtless at unexpected times of day and night. To be fair, he was from another part of the world and a bit incomprehensible in both speech and habits, so the God comparison wasn't entirely unwarranted. This neighbor looked like a leaner, younger version of my husband. This should have flattered my husband. That the hand I felt during my only moments of relief belonged in a sense to an idealized version of my husband. This did not make him happy, however. His response was to cover the bedroom windows overlooking the neighbor's garden with a translucent adhesive that imitated etched glass and made psychedelic rainbow patterns of sunlight on my prickling legs as I lay on the bed and masturbated to imagined scenes with my neighbor because I didn't really need to see him IRL to conjure him, so it was yet another example of my husband's powerlessness, which did not ease the building tension in our house.

"What makes you think there's a barrier you're even missing?" asked my best friend who felt for me, though not too much.

"There's got to be," I said, "like a blood-brain barrier." I tried to sound jaunty when I said that, since she was the kind of best friend who didn't respond kindly to desperation, which, under non-desperate circumstances, I agreed with.

"Crossed," she said, shaking her head. "All the time."

"So . . . what?" I said, "It's not a thing?" If I could not identify the missing boundary, how could I rebuild it?

"Semipermeable," she said, "like everything else. You feel therefore you are," she added, patting my thigh. Her hand on my thigh felt terrible.

The fifth doctor believed the cure was to avoid the feelings. "Think," he said. "You cannot think and feel at the same time."

I told him I thought I could.

"Try," he said.

I felt the doctor's arrogance: a dry, hard ball in my solar plexus, so I turned it into a thought. I would like to kill this doctor, I thought, but the dry, hard ball I felt in my solar plexus only grew larger.

"Do not try to turn the feeling into a thought," said the doctor, demonstrating that he could think about how I might mistake his advice. "*Think* about the feeling instead of feeling it."

I thought about the dry, hard ball in my solar plexus, how it was twin to the damp, empty hole I felt in my heart. Then I thought about the damp, empty hole—how it had first opened when I was ten, and I tried to explain to my mother that other people scared me even though I knew there was nothing to be scared of, and that I'd thought to myself, maybe they're like spiders—more afraid of me than I am of them, but that that had only made it worse, because then I saw other people as spiders with too many arms and big awful eyes, and my mother had put her hand on my head and said, "You think too much," and a space opened up between her words and their meaning and my whole body crawled in, quaking.

"Don't thoughts lead to feelings, though?" I asked the doctor.

"Not if you don't let them," he said. I asked him what if feelings were just the body's thoughts.

"I see your wife likes to argue," said the doctor to my husband. Talking to me was difficult for this doctor because he felt that talking to me was encouraging me. I felt strongly that he felt that: an ache just behind my right eye socket. This gave me an idea. With each feeling that arose, I would greet it with a welcome. "Hello, feeling," I said to the doctor's displeasure. "Hello, feeling," I said to my husband's embarrassment. "Hello, feeling," I said to my exasperation. I knew from meditation that welcoming was a sly way of disarming. "Welcome," I said to the rage I felt as the doctor shook my husband's hand and placed his other hand on the small of my back so he could push me out the door. My rage softened and melted into little drops in the corners of my eyes.

The sidewalk outside the fifth doctor's building was crowded, and I felt excited, worried, ambivalent, guilty, scared, inadequate—strangers' feelings! This was why lately I had taken to avoiding public places. Strangers' feelings had a certain alien feel to them. They were thinner, for instance, tinnier, and were often accompanied by a mineral taste in my mouth, like when you drank water from another part of the country and it tasted like water, but different from the water you were used to. This stepping outside of yet another doctor's building after being told again how not to feel was a mouthful of wrong water.

"Do you want to be by yourself?" my husband asked that evening. He could see I was exhausted.

I shook my head. "*No*," I said, "I just want to be *myself*."

"As in, not someone else?"

"As in, not everyone else."

He paused. Looked at me sitting on the couch, my arms outstretched, my body like a piece of hide strung between two trees, drying in the sun. "Maybe it's time to accept that we're all connected?" he said. He said it like that. Upward inflecting: connected? This was new. I felt a softening in my jaw. His softening. What had he been reading, I asked, because I knew his feelings were affected by what and whom he read. "Natalie Moon," he said. "She calls herself a witch." Where I expected to feel his scorn, there was something new. A lump in my chest: his hopefulness. "I mean," he said, "we've tried everything else."

Natalie Moon: *Mentor, guide, magician,* said her website. She listed certifications I was not familiar with and after her name were initials I did not recognize. Nevertheless, I liked her photograph: a forty-something woman standing by an oak tree with long brown hair and a frank expression. She looked straight at the camera, her mouth upturned in the slightest smile, and the hint of a botanical tattoo peeked above the neckline of her sweater. I emailed her that night, listing my symptoms, my history, and everything I'd tried. "I'm just so tired of feeling everything. And I mean everything," I concluded.

Several upcoming sessions were fully booked, but she invited me to join her next available workshop to be held over a long weekend in three months' time. Her apparent popularity was encouraging.

"What kind of workshop?"

"Feel Better Immersion," she wrote back. I marked my calendar.

That night I was deeply agitated, my over-feeling was worsening to the point of unendurable, and for the first time, masturbation did no good, so I enlisted my husband. He helped. In fact, he helped so well, he began to help daily, then twice daily, which was a great thing, until the inevitable occurred: One early morning I felt a fattened ovum plant itself on an inner left wall of my body, followed by a coppery weight on my tongue like a penny. I was pregnant.

Not that we hadn't tried to avoid the inevitable. The night before we got engaged, my husband had a vasectomy. We'd agreed. It was wrong to bring children into this world, though we had different reasons. His were mostly environmental—the climate crisis, pollution, etc. Mine were more emotional—teeming with both vulnerability and cruelty, children terrified me. For half a dozen years, we'd avoided conception.

Then, on its own, my husband's vas deferens reattached. That was a term we hadn't spoken until his doctor pronounced it so definitively. Then we couldn't speak it enough. As if repeating vas deferens could reverse the reversal of the vasectomy. As if reversing the reversal of the vasectomy could reverse the pregnancy that had resulted.

"What should we watch tonight?"

"Vas deferens."

"Do you want hemp or oat milk in your coffee?"

"Vas deferens."

"What does it even mean, vas deferens?" I asked.

My husband looked it up: carrying-away vessel.

"Your carrying-away vessel got carried away!"

"Who got carried away?" said my husband, peering at me over his glasses.

"Vas deferens," I said with a shrug.

Despite the stab at levity, I was not casual about the new state of my person. Not at all. Already I could barely contain all the feelings of my own body and those bodies around me. Now I could add to the overabundance of symptoms: pain in my lower back, dizziness, and weakness. Soon I was going to feel nauseous and then exhausted and then tender, hot, bloated, constipated, crampy, wet-mouthed, gassy, hungry, sleepless, blurry, swollen, forgetful, and breathless. And that was all *before* giving birth.

The sixth doctor, an OBGYN, performed a sonogram and announced that my fertilized egg was in my left fallopian tube and that since a tubal pregnancy was a nonviable pregnancy and could be fatal if not addressed quickly, the treatment was to end the pregnancy. I felt a great relief. Greater still because I felt it shared with my husband. The doctor administered an injection of medication, and I immediately felt an internal pause: a halt in cell growth. The nurse warned that I might feel mild cramping over the next week and could expect some light vaginal bleeding. "Your body will absorb the remaining tissue," she added.

"You're lucky to live in this state," the doctor said as I rose from the table. However, I didn't feel lucky so much as anxious and sad. It was the OBGYN's anxiety (a constriction at my right temple) and the nurse's sadness (an ache in my bones), though it was not clear if what they were feeling was about me, my ectopic pregnancy, or the state of their profession.

By the time I arrived at Natalie Moon's Feel Better Immersion, all I felt was everything but pregnant again. There were six of us. All women. We sat on pillows on the floor around Natalie's coffee table which was piled with acorns, leaves, and stones. Natalie lit a beeswax candle, and as we passed it from hand to hand she said, nodding to each of us in turn, "You began as a feeling between two people." This felt like a nod to my ill-fated pregnancy, which I found distracting. When the candle returned to her, she added, "We all did." It quickly became apparent that Feel Better Immersion was not a workshop aimed at healing any ailment, but a training session for feeling skillfully. Not feel *better*, but *feel* better.

"You each possess a power," Natalie said as she released us blindfolded over her yard. "Be like the paramecium," she said. "Witness your conjugation." My embarrassment was matched only by my curiosity. Following her instructions, we rustled around in the leaves until we found one another and then lay down on the grass in a circle with our heads at the center. Then Natalie began to hum, and filaments of our selves stretched out, united, and exchanged. Bits of each for bits of the other—a new scrap of joy, a new sorrow.

By dinnertime, it was clear I was the least accomplished feeler of the group. Julie could feel what animals in a quarter-mile radius around her felt, including, but not limited to, her dogs, her neighbors' chinchilla, field mice, squirrels, chipmunks, raccoons, and the occasional still-live lobster. Ynez felt the feelings of actors and newscasters whenever she watched them on television. Shawna felt the feelings of anyone who'd lived within the past fifty years in whatever space she occupied. Shaquanna felt hurricanes, tornadoes, and earthquakes from hundreds of miles away. Zoya felt the inner life of trees.

Initially, realizing that what I felt as too much was still so much less than what these women felt made me feel better. A feeling I recognized from my visits to hospitals and waiting rooms. However, soon the relative relief of not feeling as much as the other women gave way to a new agitation over my inadequacy as a feeler. Nervous and disoriented, I slipped skittishly along the continuum of how I felt about my feelings.

"The world must be felt," Natalie said as she sent us to bed that first night, and duly, I dreamed that everything in the world was made of thick, soft cloth, matted and pressed.

Natalie Moon's methods were rigorous and experiential, and during the course of the long weekend, I slowly warmed to her conviction that expanding one's feeling capability was a radical act benefiting not only oneself, but the entire planet.

During the three days, I learned to feel: magnetic north by the pressure in my inner ear; the exhalation of ancestors along the top of my scalp; along a wall for studs and also the hollows dug by termites; patterns of airwaves across my fingertips from an elevated pulse across a room; the weight of the dew on grass; the pressure of a secret; the glee of the rain; the tension in a sunrise.

Perhaps most useful, though, was that Natalie taught us to differentiate between feelings and gave us systems for storing them, so we'd know which ones to pay attention to and when—color coding the mellow blues from the urgent reds; taste coding the needy, acidic feelings vs. the patient, syrupy ones. It did not matter whether what we felt was our feeling or someone else's, whether it belonged to a person or an animal or a plant, only whether the feeling needed immediate attention and if so, what kind. The day we left, I felt better than I'd felt in years. Which is to say, a dawning confidence alongside the growing thrum.

On the drive home, everything wanted to feel. The wind palmed the windshield, the car wheels pawed the rutted road, traffic lights poked at the passing day. On the radio every story made its claim: the climate, the war, the court ruling, the virus, the election, the refugees, the contamination, the prisons. And through it all, my body pulsed with Natalie's parting words: "Make yourself felt."

HALF-LiVES

THIS IS A TRUE story. All the strangest stories are.

While inside my mother's uterus, I had a twin. Identical. Formed of the same egg, divided. At first everything was fine. Then I engulfed her, took her over. I was born with her inside my abdomen. Now this fetus in fetu inside me is neither alive nor dead. The doctors can't say. When they try, they look at their hands and talk incomprehensibly about fetiform masses, dermoid cysts, and mature teratomas.

My fetus in fetu cannot be removed. It is too intricately connected to the workings of my body. Its blood is my blood.

I've researched my rare condition. There isn't a lot out there. Fewer than ninety known cases in medical history. Here's what I know: The fetus in fetu has no prospect of any life outside of its host. Moreover, it poses clear threats to the life of the host twin on whom its own life depends.

In a YouTube video I watched, astrophysicist Neil deGrasse Tyson talks about Stupid Design: "Most places in the universe will kill life instantly. . . . Just look at the volume of the universe where you can't live. . . . That's not what I call the Garden of Eden. . . . Ninety-nine percent . . . of all life that has ever lived is now extinct. The inner solar system is a shooting gallery—comets, asteroids, duck!"

I have a name for this fetus in fetu. I call it the Hydra. Mythic swamp creature, toxic breath, poisonous blood, nine indestructible heads at first—but when one is severed two more grow back.

I am the dominant twin, but she is the boss of me. As long as the Hydra is dormant, I live a relatively normal life. If it grows, I am in trouble.

Here's what it looks like: It's got legs and arms, fingers and toes, a head and hair, genitals, and a vague approximation of a face. Yes, it has fingernails.

Had things gone differently she'd be sitting here with me now, wearing a dress like mine, maybe with a different haircut, but otherwise looking, talking, thinking exactly like me. A sandgoby's response to a slowly hatching egg is to eat it. Baboons have been known to eat their young. I too am an animal.

What I am is host to my parasitic twin. How I look is normal. Still, my hosting body causes me problems. I have stomach pains, shortness of breath, high blood pressure, headaches, heartburn, constipation, palpitations, insomnia, fatigue. I have a high tolerance for pain. The Hydra makes it hard to sleep, hard to climb stairs, hard to run after a piece of paper that's blown out of my hand. Sometimes I feel as if my skin is tearing as it stretches.

In my job, I am a middle school humanities teacher. Poetry, ancient civilizations. I write my students notes in terza rima. They write back in palindromes. I show slides from my trip to Rome, tell my students I put my hand in the Bocca della Verità. "I must not be a liar," I say, since my hand was not bitten off.

I have taught at the Beecham Sackner School for eight years. After my first year, the headmistress told the middle school director, "Give Lexy anything she wants." I have a way with kids.

There's a theory that teachers work with students at the age when they themselves were happiest. In sixth grade I was the second tallest girl in the school; my boyfriend read me comic books over the phone; I won first place in the hurdles at the track meet; for Halloween, I was a hooker—wrap skirt, high heels, hoop earrings, lipstick. Everything was ahead of me.

No one but my doctors know. And they are sworn to secrecy. Physician-patient privilege. I will never be closer to anyone than I am to my unformed twin.

This is what secrecy does. It sleeps three seconds later than you, so when you wake—for a moment—you are a free woman in an open world. Then secrecy grabs you around the throat again. Secrecy has clammy hands that warm as the day goes on—warm against your skin, so by the afternoon you hardly notice them on your neck. Secrecy has a sense of humor, preferring puns and double entendres. Secrecy likes to answer the phone, then pretend you are not home. Secrecy loves parties—is the first to arrive and the last to leave. Secrecy is a closeted exhibitionist and lets you sing at a faculty talent show, pose topless for a photographer friend, skinny dip in a cold lake, or dress like a diva or a hippy artist, but secrecy won't let anyone swim your shark-infested moat.

I tell none of my friends. Telling would not make us closer. Love is not pity. Others might weaken and break, but I can live outside the campfire circle and still not freeze.

Six months ago, at the wedding of a childhood friend, I met a man. Small, bearded, funny. Most men find me strident. Too smart, too sure. Superior. Todd was undeterred. We spent the reception swapping theories, exchanging witticisms, leaning toward one another, dancing. Then at the end, he asked if I wanted another drink. When I drink too much the Hydra gets heavy and pulls to the side, throwing me off balance. I remain clearheaded, but my body goes numb.

"I shouldn't," I said, instinctively putting a hand on my stomach.

"Oh, wow," he said. "I mean I had no idea, congratulations." He shifted in his chair. "I thought you were single."

"I am single," I said, confused.

"Well wow, then. Good for you. I admire that. I admire you," he was leaning away from me now, looking at my body. I followed his gaze to my belly where my hand rested. Through the dress, beneath my palm, was a small but clear protrusion.

"Oh no," I said. "That's not a baby. It's just my anencephalic twin inside there." Perhaps I'd drunk more than I thought. Perhaps I figured I'd never see him again. Perhaps I thought a joke could make it impossible.

"I don't get it," he said. "What does that mean?"

"Brainless," I said. Meaning the meaning. Meaning the Hydra. Meaning myself for talking, for fooling myself, for thinking I could be normal even for an evening.

There is a part of us that always wishes to come clean. A murderer leaves behind a fingerprint, a bank robber writes his demands on the back of his subpoena, a doctor tells a patient she'll be all right but doesn't blink once.

I braced myself for what would necessarily follow: fear, disgust, pity.

Finally, he said, "So when's it due?"

What I saw was a very long, very dark corridor, and at the end, a door. "Five months," I said. Everyone else talks about what's inside them. Everyone else moves on.

I rode the train home in my black dress and sunglasses. I could have been going to a secret rendezvous. I could have been running from a torrid love affair. I could have been on the lam, meeting an accomplice. Glamorous and alone—an amnesiac movie star forgetting what movie she was in—I examined the new lump of my stomach. I told myself it was the angle at which I was sitting, told myself it was all the wedding food. The light, the drape of the dress, the cut of the fabric. It was, in fact, the Hydra beginning to grow.

A clarification: I am not one of the truly unlucky. The truly unlucky is the Afghan man too poor to pay the bribe for the death certificate for his son—killed by a suicide bomber who wasn't targeting him, but rather the Canadian peacekeepers who got away. The truly unlucky is Andrés Escobar, accidentally scoring the winning goal against his own team at a World Cup game, gunned down in a parking lot ten days later, his murderer shouting "Goal!" with each shot.

When the doctors first told me about the Hydra—sonogrammed and scanned me, blood-tested and palpated me—they said I could die. They put me in a white gown and wheeled me from CAT scan machine to X-ray machine. At first, they were star students in love with a challenge—they walked briskly into the room, clipboards at the ready. They examined MRIs, took biopsies, and listened. One doctor smelled the back of my neck. Another brought in an acupuncturist who checked my tongue and shook her head. But soon they grew despondent. I stumped them all. "This is one of those things in medical science we have very little experience with," one doctor said. He looked at a spot somewhere just above my head, as if addressing Saint Luke himself, patron saint of doctors, students, butchers, and artists. That was two years ago. Still, I'm here. At any moment I might get sick and die. How does that make me different?

I have researched ways to slow the Hydra's growth— avoid dairy, exercise daily, take echinacea, ginseng, propolis. I have defied odds before: accepted by five Ivy League schools, maintained my virginity past thirty, rolled four Yahtzees in a row. Everyone is betting on something. This will be the same.

At my school, the science department scheduled a class trip to the local nuclear power plant, and I was asked to co-chaperone by Carla, the science chair. She knew if I came, the kids would want to come. The students couldn't stop talking about it. Lauren wanted to know if they would get nuked. Molly asked what would happen if there was a leak. Sam wondered if the lunch would glow. Cameron asked whether they would get to wear a special suit.

The girls were terrified, the boys excited. One boy told the girls that if they went, they'd grow up to have two-headed babies with gills.

Like all good teachers, I secretly have a favorite student. Cordelia falls asleep at her desk. I watch her eyelids drooping, her head falling and catching as she tries to stay awake. After class one day, I asked her what time she goes to bed at night. She told me bedtime feels like a punishment, an endless timeout she can never work off and has to repeat every single day. I told her the myth of Sisyphus—as if going to bed surrounded by people who knew and loved you could be an eternal torture.

So, I chaperoned a trip to a nuclear power plant with my least favorite coworker and a dull pressure in my temples. I sat on the bus next to Cordelia, who asked if it were possible to die of loneliness. And I wondered, was this a test or just another question? I watched the city shrink and flatten to a postcard at the back of the bus. The river thumped its bare feet outside my window, tapped at the docks and rocks, and I thought maybe outside the city I could live a happy life. Maybe I should move to where the world slips in easily over welcome mats.

And then, with a flick of its spiked tail, the Hydra suggested I remember who I was, that I did not subscribe to the commonplace or the easy, that I had chosen secrecy over talk show revelation. That inside me, there were cords that led nowhere, hair atop nothing. That I was overrun with nerves.

The bus pulled up to a security gate and the boys behind me couldn't help kicking at my seat. They saw the armed guard and the military vehicle parked just inside the perimeter.

"This is so cool," one of them said. A razor line of pain ran up my side—the Hydra's way of telling me I was not

alone. It wouldn't give me loved or protected, so I settled
for not alone because this was the evil I knew, this was the
scared I was used to. Because I hadn't the time to figure
out another way just now, not while I was responsible for
half a busload of children wanting to know everything.

First, we were ushered into a building where we
signed papers. We disavowed drugs and alcohol—the children smirked, looked side to side, promised to hold onto
railings, not to breach the motion-activated double fence,
not to splash in puddles, kick at ice, or step off the path
and run. Our names were called, and our identity cards
were distributed. We lined up and walked through a metal
detector, then a weapons detector. Green lights for all. I
felt a torque inside me, an unfurling. It was the Hydra saying, undetected did not mean gone.

Next, we were taken to a darkened conference room
where a senior information specialist greeted us and
gave us a PowerPoint presentation. The children fidgeted,
tapped the tables, picked their scalps. Bright slides flashed
the words SAFE, SECURE, VITAL.

"What's vital?" Lauren asked Ava.

Ava said, "You know, what you can die from. Like vital
signs."

The lights went on and the senior information specialist asked for questions. The children were prepared.
They asked about risks, dangers, contamination, leaks.
They quoted environmentalists, activists, politicians. The
man kept to his script—facility upgrades, expert planning,

community contributions, clean energy. "What happens when you run out of storage for all the spent fuel?" Leo wanted to know. The man smiled, talked about reinforced steel and concrete walls two-feet thick, underground fuel pools, and dry cask storage.

The room smelled like corkboard and ozone. Half presentation, half odor control. Like a pregnant woman I have a preternatural sense of smell, but mostly what I smell is my body. Not just the musk of my armpits and the funk between my legs, but the lumps inside my belly button, the breath on my upper lip, my earwax, my scalp sweat, even the insides of my nostrils. I smell my body everywhere.

A blindfolded mycologist can identify a fungus by its odor alone; an endocrinologist knows ketoacidosis by the Juicy Fruit perfume of his patient's breath; a dog sniffs his owner's impending seizure minutes before it happens.

What is a tour without a promotional movie? What is a promotional movie without 3D glasses? It took little to make this captive audience happy—cellophane glasses, a brochure with a smiling woman in a hard hat. The lights went out again and the movie, *A Flying Tour of the Exelergy Nuclear Power Facility*, lasted twelve minutes, had a 3D talking kangaroo and shots of the Exelergy company "family" playing softball and badminton. The river was blue, the sky was clear. After the movie there was an Exelergy Quiz. Students won prize: stickers, handkerchiefs, and mini Post-its, all decorated with the Exelergy kangaroo.

If the Hydra had a gift shop, here's what it would sell: a tea specially designed to leave a leafy skull and cross-bones at the bottom of your cup when you're finished; a hologram of Alfred Hitchcock that walks into the frame of your life at unexpected moments, reminding you your story is a suspense thriller prone to mistaken identity and double-crosses; mugs with ultrasound images of headless embryos; magic grow pellets of mini babies which expand in water to ten times their dry size and smell like rotting carrion; DON'T ASK, DON'T TELL buttons; everything in maroon.

The senior information specialist handed us off to a tour guide who walked us outside into the sun. Just then Carla leaned into me and said, "Know what Dan Becker of the Sierra Club said? He said switching from coal to nukes is like giving up smoking and taking up crack." I told her in that case I could see the appeal. I don't like Carla. She gives her students A's for telling her what she's told them; she thinks prepared is the same as smart.

The tour guide stopped in front of a concrete building and held up a capsule the size of the tip of her finger. "One pellet of uranium is equal to one ton of coal, 149 gallons of oil, 17,000 cubic feet of gas," she said. It was her youngest child and she was proud of all the little squirt could do.

"Is the uranium inside that?" asked one of the students.

"Oh no," she said. "This is just a model. The real uranium pellets are stacked into fuel rods, put into fuel assemblies. There are 764 assemblies plus 185 control rods standing 15 feet tall in the reactor core." The tour guide, like uranium, was primitive—the bigger the number the more impressive.

What the tour guide didn't say about uranium: more common than tin, with a half-life of 4.5 billion years, it is a geologic original sin so unstable that it's constantly shedding a part of itself. The women who painted the glow-in-the-dark numbers on the watch faces at the US Radium Corporation in New Jersey in the 1920s also painted their nails with the uranium paint. They licked their brushes, licked their fingers. Their teeth fell out, abscesses grew in their jaws, their bodies filled with cancer, and they died.

Criticism, the middle school head often tells us, should be given in the form of a sandwich—praise, suggestion, praise. Critique: the lean deli slice between two thick halves of a bun. I go for high protein, low carb. Ask me what I think, and I'll give you the meat—gristle, blood, marbled fat. I am not a bakery. I do not dispense muffins and cakes.

Next, we were taken to a room where a man had a rack of protective suits for the students to practice putting on. He presented the strict protocols for behavior in contaminated areas and then pointed out the violations each student accidentally committed. There was a way to put the suits on and a way to take them off. A handheld meter ran over their pubescent hands, checking for tiny radioactive spots.

We are in constant danger: a giant asteroid, a speeding car, a falling tree, a stray bullet, to say nothing of the eco-apocalypse. Still we leave our houses, still we walk the streets, still we get on a bus and go on a trip.

My job on this trip was crowd control. The science teachers had made up worksheets the students filled in as they toured the plant. I was there to keep them focused, to keep the girls from clumping into groups, from whispering, and to keep the boys from tripping one another, mumbling curses under their breath. The job was simple.

"They wouldn't take us here if it were dangerous," I heard Ava say to Lauren as we followed the tour guide toward a second building. "Their job is to keep us safe."

I have never been able to keep anything safe. Houseplants wilt and die in my care. Goldfish mottle and gray and then float in my bowls. I subbed for the recess lady when she had the flu and a child got hit in the forehead with a rock. She walked up to me with her hand over the hole, and when I looked in all I could see was bone, blood, and darkness for a mile.

The tour guide took us into the control room. It was something from a movie set—dials, lights, diagrams, meters, and banks of warning lights neatly packed together on the lit ceiling. There was a table in the middle where one man sat, and two other workers—a man and a woman—stood at opposite ends of the room, moving between screens and panels. The man at the table looked up as we walked in.

"Welcome to the brain of the operation," he said. I didn't know if he meant himself or the control room. Either way, I was not impressed.

The students looked back and forth from me to the tour guide, unsure what kind of channel the TV had been switched to. Not Disney, but not Discovery either. One or two of the students stifled a laugh; the others took a wait-and-see approach. The tour guide continued, not missing a beat. She told us three people were at the control board on twelve-hour shifts around the clock, running tests, logging measurements—busy, busy, highly trained.

I had not turned in my 3D glasses, so I took them out of my bag and put them on. All at once the walls, covered with switches, indicators, recorders, and lights, were a firework of colored dashes, and everything sat flat. I liked the glasses. Carla and the power plant workers were characters in a Looney Tunes short—nervous, squashed, impotent. The room was full of light and color, and everything was beautiful.

"What's that glowing stuff?" Leo asked, pointing to a picture on a monitor. "That's the nuclear reaction inside the reactor core," he was told; the rods glowed as they heated the water.

"Cool!" The boys glowed too—it was exciting to see radiation. Fire, lava, tornadoes, earthquakes, tsunamis—the closer you got the longer you'd live. When I nearly tripped over Jordan's shoelaces, I took the glasses off and I wondered: Were the control room workers trained to handle an emergency of doubt? A flash of fear? A sudden surge of inexplicable helplessness?

It was nearly noon when the tour guide escorted us to a conference room on another floor. We were served room-temperature pizza, apparently delivered long ago. Pizza inspected and approved by Exelergy. I pictured the delivery man given the all clear, driving away wondering if half-lives felt like real lives, if half-lives ever ended.

"Nuclear power is safer than pizza," Lauren said. "You know how many people choke on pizza and die every year?"

Henry said, "Pizza is Italy's answer to stale bread and leftovers."

Leo said, "Nuclear pizza would glow in the dark so you could find it under your bed in the middle of the night." He grinned and showed his half-chewed food.

"Your mouth looks like a nuclear waste site," said Ava. Then Erin—who is new this year from a fancy uptown school—said that for her, nuclear waste is a used Q-tip whose end is slathered with orange ear cheese and you can't tell if the other end is still usable. You can't flush it without clogging the toilet, and if you put it in the trash, the whole bathroom smells like the inside of someone else's head.

The other students paused, considered whether Erin was more creative or only better at getting attention. Henry burped and they all rolled their eyes. Then Cordelia said her father said the world is full of things you want

to throw away but can't, and she started to list them: cau-
liflower, the carpet your little brother puked on, your little
brother, the video of you running naked through the house
screaming, "I poop! I poop!" I envied her her list.

When I strangled the Hydra in a dream last night, it wasn't
the eyes—which it doesn't have—that popped out, but
the heart—which it also doesn't have—huge and red and
pumping hard. And when it did, that heart said in Leonard
Nimoy's voice, which is how I knew I was dreaming, "This
is highly illogical."

After lunch the tour guide returned with hard hats, goggles, and earplugs, and she led us into the reactor building,
which was hot and loud. We were walked past the radioactive room: more computers, yellow and black hazard signs
posted on the walls. As if the workers might forget. As if
wearing hazmat suits and not being let out unless deemed
clean were ever-so-routine that those workers might think
this was an ordinary job where they could dress down on
Fridays or drink wine with lunch.

We looked at them through the glass: specimens on
a top-security Petri dish, working under cameras and
motion sensors, surrounded by a perimeter of armed
guards and security boats. A living experiment waiting
to go bad. When Jordan said he thought he heard an air-
plane, the tour guide smiled and told us that's impossible,
"there's a no-fly zone in the airspace within ten nautical

miles of this plant." Leo asked what happens if a plane veers into the protected airspace. Do they shoot it down?

The Hydra was quiet. In fact, since entering the inner section of the power plant the Hydra hadn't moved at all.

When an opossum is threatened it plays dead: eyes glazed, tongue lolling, teeth bared, saliva foaming; foul-smelling, stiff, curled, breath-stifled, heart slowed. You prod it, you poke it—nothing. Turn, shake, or lift it— still nothing. An opossum playing dead won't give itself up.

We were led into a vast and empty room. "We are standing on the refueling floor directly over the reactor vessel," the tour guide shouted. Her eyes shone. The children looked down at their feet, as if they were about to light up. She couldn't stop talking about the highly trained *injuneers*. Like we were guests at a Halloween party given by the Nuclear Regulatory Commission and everyone was invited: Scalped Injuns, dead presidents, Lizzie Borden, Dr. Strangelove. I looked at the kids and they were all cherubs and putti, and somewhere Caravaggio was running around with his paintbrushes and his dirty fingernails trying to get one of the boys alone.

"This plant has been in operation since 1990," she said. The mention of the year jarred me. It was as old as I was. Everything hummed and shook and the noise through the earplugs wouldn't stop.

The tour guide talked on, simultaneously passing out maps and diagrams—about redundant protection systems, defense in depth, barriers, containment, zirconium, steel. In my hand I held a cutaway drawing of the reactor core. It looked like a body during an autopsy—skin flayed, muscle peeled back, innards revealed.

Bodies have lives of their own. In a forty-degree room, sheets drenched in cold water are draped over the shoulders of Tibetan monks in meditation. Instead of shivering, the monks begin to sweat. Steam rises from the wet sheets and within an hour they are dry. A group of seventy-year-olds is isolated in an environment replicating 1959—decor, music, magazines. Within a week, signs of aging reverse: Their joints become flexible, their posture straightens, their fingers lengthen, their eyesight improves.

"You are here," the tour guide shouted at us, pointing to the primary map. "During a refueling outage," she continued, "this floor is transformed into a highly choreographed work zone. Workers climb into the reactor vessel to conduct repairs." Then she paused and asked us to picture people in full protective suits wiping the nodes of the fuel assemblies, operators on headsets watching glowing screens, everyone circling the robot guts—greasing, oiling, cleaning, adjusting. The children stood still, picturing, entering the fantasy. They were awed by the noise and the heat and the size of everything. She could have told them their tongues were swelling to twice their size and they'd have panicked, suddenly unable to speak.

The weird smile on the tour guide's face, the closed-hamper smell of the children's hair, and this garish map in my hand made me dizzy. The room was hot and loud, and I felt I might be sick. I put my hand out and steadied myself on a pipe; the tour guide told me to please refrain from touching any of the equipment. She asked me to stay to the side, to watch my purse as we rounded the corner, to follow her lead. I wanted to punch her.

This morning Leo forgot his coat when he left his house. Just before the bus pulled away from the school his mother came running up with it. "I just want to say," she said to Carla in the bus doorway, "what you are doing is so good for these kids. Showing them both sides of an issue, letting them come to their own conclusion." Carla beamed and said something pat about critical thinking and lifelong learning. She could be a mascot for fair and balanced.

"If radioactive waste could talk, what would it say?" I asked our tour guide.

"Excuse me?" she smiled.

"I was just wondering," I said. Cordelia looked up, tilted her head to see me through the goggles on her nose. "From the perspective of the nuclear power company, would you say the glowing waste would tell us it is misunderstood?" The children began to shift where they stood, the boys pulled at their pockets, the girls' eyes widened. I could not stop myself. "Should we have sympathy for the spent fuel's lonely existence, do you think? Maybe all it really wants is to be appreciated. A little air. A chance to feel the warmth of the sun on its cheek."

It is not my job to feel empathy for what can kill me. Nor to make love to the object of my ruin. I leave that to the gurus and the Dalai Lamas. W.S. Merwin said "the present is an absolutely transparent moment that only great saints ever see occasionally."

Carla stepped forward. "She teaches poetry," she apologized. Our tour guide tried to rearrange her face to show that this explained everything. Then to the students Carla said, in a voice meant to show she was the one really in charge, "For homework tonight, please write a page in your science journals from the perspective of uranium."

The tour guide said something else about the plant's security and everyone's safety. I wanted to tell the students this was not an information tour. This was a propaganda tour. I wanted to tell them to go home and tell their parents they were subjected to the intensive brainwashing of blithe salesmen who thought they could save the world by containing all its dangers in two-feet-thick concrete. My heart was pounding, and the Hydra felt like it was stretching for a fight. Sweat was beading around my lips, dripping down my lower back.

"This power plant provides 30 percent of the power for the city you live in," the woman said, trying to smile, but stiffening so her face looked like half of it had gotten caught in a vise. I let out a laugh that probably sounded more like a bark.

"Underage workers provide 75 percent of the world's chocolate," I said. "That is not an argument for child labor." The woman was confused. Lauren and Ava started to giggle and couldn't stop. Leo had stopped tapping his notepad and was looking between me and the tour guide as though he were suddenly at an interesting sporting event. I was about to tell her she'd swallowed her own glowing Kool-Aid. I was about to tell her all kinds of things. Instead, a security guard suddenly appeared at my side and told me he was escorting me somewhere more comfortable. And just as suddenly, this sounded like a good idea.

Outside there was a cool breeze, and when I took out my earplugs the noise inside my head had stopped.

The doctors say I must remain in the best possible condition. There are bricks attached to my ankles, but still I walk. I must act as if I am normal; the more fully the actor is committed to the role, the more convincing the performance.

I never know if this heaviness in my legs is from the Hydra or my fear of it. My Hydra is insatiable, asking all of me—as if I chose to house it, as if I wouldn't cut it out and leave it, all hairy stumps and mangled limbs, in a pool of blood and mucus at the bottom of a dumpster if I could.

I looked up at the round concrete domes and the fat cylinders of steam rising into the air. What was the point of right, if you couldn't have understood?

I told the security guard it was fine; I was okay now; I'd stay outside; I could use the air. But there was no free walking around a nuclear power plant. He needed to take me back to the reception building. On the way I asked him how he liked his job. He said it was fine. The pay was good. I asked if he often had to escort someone from a tour group. He said sometimes people felt a little faint.

We walked on the designated path back to the first building, back to the room where we were shown the promotional video. The security guard opened the door for me, turned on the lights. This was where I was to wait for the rest of my group. I thought of putting on my 3D glasses again, but there was very little to see—just metal chairs and tables—even the screen had been retracted into the ceiling.

Eventually the group filed back in. Most of the students didn't bother with me, but Cordelia came right up to where I sat.

"Why did you do that?" she asked.

"I was playing a game," I said. What kind of game, she wanted to know. "It's called 'Don't Think about The Hydra and The Hydra Won't Think About You.'" Cordelia looked at me. She had the look of someone who took things seriously and cared. Like me, only younger and with promise.

I was reminded of a marine-life special I saw late one night on television: Young electric eels have good eyesight, but as they age, they become increasingly blind due to constant exposure to the electrical field they themselves generate.

"My mother said what you don't think about always gets you in the end," Cordelia told me. I said her mom was a smart woman and as such was entitled to her opinion.

If I taught what I knew I'd start my own program in Narrative Denial. Program description: The practice of denial requires a convincing narrative of entertaining bravado and odds-beating confidence. Deepen selective amnesia and extend voluntary ignorance with narrative skills such as humor and distraction. Mesmerize yourself and others while telling an engaging story. Master narrative denial to beat the humiliation of being only who you are.

I asked Cordelia what I had missed. She told me about the cooling tower where the water vapor escaped into the air. The tour guide had explained that the water was exposed to radiation, but because it had a half-life of only seven seconds, the radiation was nearly gone by the time it reached the air.

"So, I've been trying to figure out," Cordelia said, "with a half-life of seven seconds, how long until it's got no radiation at all?"

My students still think the teacher is the Great Explainer. They ask me questions and want me to explain: Why do boys have nipples? Why does your hair look best right before you cut it? Why does a box marked fragile make you want to drop it?

"You have ten feet to walk before you're out the door," I said. "If each time you move, you go half the distance to the door, how long until you're out?"

Cordelia frowned. "The halves keep getting smaller . . . but there's always more," she said.

"Right," I said. "Half-lives are never over."

On the bus ride home, kids in the back slept shoulder to shoulder, their foreheads dropping and lifting at every bump, and a day in my life disappeared behind me. The nuclear power plant was a gray dot topped with a blinking light, shrinking.

Sometimes I imagine I'm the star of a reality TV show. It makes sense: I am always either trying to survive or performing some sort of overly rehearsed feat. Everything I do has a highly competitive edge to it—the lessons I teach, the plans I make, the dreams I have, all seem to be judged by some unseen public. Later, when I review the events of my life they seem to have been manipulated through some sort of editing or other post-production technique, so that nothing seems to be the way I remember it.

"I'm glad that's over," Lauren said to Molly.

"My mom was right," said Ava. "It was perfectly safe."

"How do you know?" Leo said, twisting around to give the girls a devilish smile.

"We're alive, aren't we?" Lauren said.

"Duh. Radiation doesn't kill you instantly," said Henry.

"Yeah, it takes a while," said Sam. "In the end, you just find out you've got it, and it's too late." The girls told the boys to shut up, and so they turned back to their armpit farting contest.

Carla took the ride back as an opportunity to berate me. "It's not the children I should have worried about, it's you," Carla said. "You think you're always right."

I wanted to say, if you are always right then thinking you are is only clear thinking. I wanted to say that's called a healthy ego. There is a lot I could have said to Carla, but I was tired, and the Hydra was pulling me deeper and deeper into my seat, like someone sitting on my bowels. So, I nodded and let her go on, jabbing at me with her little words.

"You can't let anything go," she said, and I let it go. Which proved she was wrong, and I was right, which was what I wanted to tell her in the first place. "Not everything is about you," she said.

So, here, Hydra, if a life is what you want then here are fear and shame and secrets. Here is the daylight you crave, that roller coaster scream, that sharp turn into neck-wrenching sight. Here is the heart-pounding, head-aching world you want, that throw of the dice, that nauseating slide into each new day.

Across the aisle, Cordelia took out a notebook and a pencil and began to draw. She gripped the pencil and her tongue moved against the inside of her cheek as she concentrated. I leaned over and asked her what she was drawing.

"A self-portrait of myself," she said.

"Can you," I said, "draw a self-portrait of anyone else?" She smiled as if to say, of course you could.

PLURAL LiKE THE UNIVERSE

Sê plural como o universo!
—*Fernando Pessoa*

TODAY IN VENICE I am a married woman. My husband is at a business conference. That's what I tell the American couple I meet in the art gallery near the Peggy Guggenheim Museum. There is nothing more plausible than a married woman.

She is ogling a series of forest-scapes displayed on the wall, which upon closer look, are formed entirely of Hebrew letters. Her brown hair is pulled back in a low ponytail and her earrings glitter in the light. Her husband is reading the painter's bio aloud from the gallery catalog, ". . . born in Padua, educated in Bologna, student of Umberto Eco . . ."

Both of their faces glisten with sweat. They are not used to Italian air conditioning.

"Ah yes, you can see that," I say. The man looks up from the catalog. "The semiotician in him, I mean."

"Where you from?" he asks.

I've shot too high. I think maybe Washington, but say instead, "Westchester."

"Get out!" the woman says. "Which town?"

I pick Armonk. They claim Ardsley. It moves along from there.

I tell them my name is Anita because I am thinking about Anita Berber, "Weimar Berlin's Priestess of Depravity," when we meet. Berber was a dancer, silent-film actress, model, and cabaret star, known to spend nights touring elegant hotels and restaurants wearing nothing but a sable coat, an antique brooch filled with cocaine, and her pet monkey around her neck. As Petrarch understood: If you got free by any strange behavior . . .

Neither Lori nor Peter speaks any Italian. This gives me an advantage. I talk to everyone who crosses our path— the gallery owner remembers me from an opening earlier in the week; a restaurant manager asks after my husband who, in his animated attempt to speak like a native, spilled wine all over his shirt there last night; a jeweler wants to know how I like my new ring.

The words Häagen-Dazs mean nothing. They're simply the vaguely Danish-sounding nonsense words invented by the ice cream's Polish American creator in an effort to come up with something original. Frusen Glädjé, on the other hand, is Swedish for frozen happiness. Briefly a competitor of Häagen-Dazs, the Frusen Glädjé brand has since disappeared, proving the feel of a thing is often more compelling than the truth of it.

"We discovered him in the ghetto," Lori says, meaning the painter whose print they just bought.

Peter wears a gold Star of David around his neck. I tell them my aunt was saved from the Nazis on the Kindertransport. They tell me the Jews saved Venice from the plague by inventing the quarantine.

It's the three of us at an outdoor table at the foot of the Accademia Bridge. Vaporetti come and go. There is a breeze, but we suck up the boats' exhaust anyway.

Peter leaves to use the bathroom. Lori begins the girl talk. She tells me she loves my dress. That she could never wear such a thing—she's too straight and flat-chested, she says. I tell her it's a matter of imagination, that she has the order wrong. First you eat the fruit, then you examine the hunger. She laughs and says she should probably eat more fruit. I tell her I made the dress. I'll send her the pattern.

"Oh, I'm not that artistic or handy or whatever it is that you are that I'm not." Then she talks about her twins. A boy and girl at home with her parents. I picture them alternately as rare earth elements and tropical fish.

When Peter returns, I make a point of seeing him as Lori does. He has a particular physical draw: that of a man who must have always been attractive, but never quite believed it. Added to this, his hair is beginning to recede, and he has the slightest intimations of a gut. I sit facing the water, flanked by Peter and his wife.

Lori leans forward and says, "So what, exactly, do you do?"

In the past I have been a braille translator, a furniture tester, a phone psychic, a makeup artist, a feng shui consultant, a puppeteer. Today I am a glass sculptor.

"Ah, Murano," she says. I nod.

"What kind of sculpture do you make?" Peter asks.

"Right now, I'm doing a series of masks based on the eight primary emotions," I say.

"That's all there are?" Lori says.

"Men have only three," Peter says. "Happy, sad, and angry."

"What about trust?" Lori says.

"Trust is an emotion?" Peter says. Then turning to me: "At law school they told us it was property held by one party for the benefit of another."

Lori rolls her eyes.

"Plus, disgust, anticipation, and . . . fear," she says.

"But what's the eighth?" She's keeping track.

"Surprise," I say.

The world is full of surprises—ugly vegetables that taste good; cacti that bloom only one night a year; women who, with a puff of breath, send men tumbling. I can take a man, shrink him, and carry him to the desert in the palm of my hand. It's a matter of balance. It's an artist's trick. Chiaroscuro, the Italians call it, the play of light and shadow.

Now it is my turn to excuse myself. I squeeze past the waiter and head inside the restaurant. Just before leaving the light, I turn. The two of them are alone at the table. They do not see me watching. My empty chair is a vacuum between them, a hole they could fall through. The canal water glistens in the space, shining so bright you can't look at it without burning a bright spot in your vision. Their hands are on the table, their bodies drawn closer to my seat, toward the chair I have vacated.

In a study of exotic dancers conducted at the University of New Mexico, researchers looked at tips earned on 5,300 lap dances and found ovulating dancers earned nearly twice as much as menstruating dancers. I am smack-dab in the middle of my cycle.

When the check arrives, Peter insists on paying. I resist.

"In fact, when I ran into you, I had just finished meeting with the manager of the Guggenheim Museum shop.

They are going to carry four of my masks," I tell them. "So, lunch is my treat."

"Congratulations!" Lori says.

Peter wants to see my masks. I tell him I left the samples at the museum but promise to send them a link to my website as soon as it's updated. In the meantime, I pull out my phone and flip through some photos I took the other day at an exhibit in a small gallery on the Giudecca. I find a picture of a ceiling hung with multicolored glass bulbs and tell them it's my studio. It's the Biennale so there's plenty of art to go around.

"You're an artist; I insist," Peter says as he signs the bill for lunch.

Apollo Robbins gets paid to pick pockets and then return the loot. He's billed as a gentleman thief and an entertainer, but really, he's a master of human attention. Like him, I know what people notice and what they don't.

"Oh God, that was bad," Lori says, rising from her chair and sitting back down again, hand pressed to her hip. She is white.

"Again?" Peter says, looking suddenly exhausted.

"You make it seem like I enjoy the pain, Peter." Lori rubs her hip with the palm of her hand. "I've had it on and off for a year or so," she says to me. "Usually I can control it with stretching. It's just that the beds in Italy are so hard and I think I've aggravated it again." I go over to where Lori's sitting and put my hand on her lower back.

"Do you feel anything here?" I ask. She jumps and then relaxes into my palm.

"That's so weird. I think you did something. It feels better." She rises. We walk a few paces. "Are you some kind of witch?" she says.

"I went to massage school in an earlier life," I smile. "I know my anatomy."

"Oh, could I use a massage," Lori says, turning to face me.

"Come back to our hotel with us, Anita," Peter says, "and give Lori a massage."

"I was never certified," I say.

"We won't sue."

I massage a naked Lori on the bed. Peter watches.

In Berlin, there's a nonprofit group called Fuck for Forest, which sells access to their erotic photos and films and donates 80 percent of the proceeds to protect the rainforest. There are a thousand ways to justify what we want.

Lori decides to take a nap. Peter decides to go look at more paintings; he walks with me to the door. "That's an interesting tattoo you have," he says just as we reach the hall. I've pulled my hair up and he's staring at the gnarled tree on the back of my neck.

"It's a bristlecone pine," I say, "the oldest single living organism known."

"How old?" Peter says.

"Upward of forty-nine hundred years," I say.

"Wish I knew its secret," Peter says.

"The harsh environment in which it grows," I say.

At the entrance to the Accademia, instead of going in, Peter keeps walking.

"I know who you remind me of," he says. I look like every man's high school girlfriend. I tilt my head and wait, pretending to be intrigued. "Veronica Lodge."

I pause. Usually I've heard of everyone.

"Archie Comics," Peter says with a smile.

Just then I trip on a raised stone and fall hard into Peter's chest. Peter holds me a moment longer than is necessary.

About 92 percent of all communication is nonverbal—air puffs, hand gestures, body tilts, nostril flares, eyebrow jumps. In other words, people transmit meaning to one another in a system worked out when we were apes.

I tell Peter I have the key to a friend's apartment. He does not bother to question this or anything else I say. His mouth is red with longing; he seeks me with open lips. I mark my territory with little bites all down his stomach. I have stolen love's body.

Afterward Peter dozes on my bed. I sketch him. Naked and postcoital, he looks like a boy. Peter Pan, I title the drawing and tuck it in his pants pocket.

We meet up with Lori late in the afternoon at the gelateria behind their hotel, as planned. Peter and I smell of each other, but only to each other. We are all rested. Sitting on the steps of a small footbridge eating our gelato, we watch a young woman walk by in a skirt and hat made of pink tulle.

"Doesn't she look like a wedding cake?" Lori says.

Soon the whole street is flooded with people talking and laughing, fanning themselves. The armpits and backs of their shirts are stained with sweat. They are all in their twenties, and there is something intensely alive about them, as if they are walking along some preordained path toward their own greatness.

"Get a load of this guy," Peter says as a young man, naked but for a large diaper and a mortarboard, parades by. He is flanked by a girl in a tuxedo and another dressed as a ladybug.

"Graduation," I say. "The university is around the corner. They're walking from the ceremony to their piazza parties."

"Piazza parties?" Lori asks.

I rise to join the current of people, and with a tilt of my head, Peter, then Lori, follows.

I like the feeling of ignorance that being not Italian gives me, the outsider status that can never be breached, despite knowing the language, despite having lived here longer than anywhere else. In the States I am forever filled with an irritated arrogance. Italy is a relief.

At the end of an alley there is a tarp on the ground. Standing on the tarp is a young woman in a bikini and rain boots reading aloud from a scroll as her friends and family cheer and heckle. The young woman hesitates, and the crowd goes wild. Someone tilts a bottle of wine toward her and the first few drops fall on her chest before her lips meet the bottle and she takes a swig. Then someone else dumps a bag of flour over her head. Everybody laughs, including the girl.

Suddenly, a louder whooping from around a corner. The crowd moves on and again we are off. I feel Peter's eyes on my body.

Around more corners, the street opens onto another piazza, and here it is a boy—naked but for his underpants, into the back of which whipped cream is being sprayed from a can. He is swaying; his friends are all cheering.

Peter maneuvers so he is standing between Lori and me. I shift slightly, so his arm grazes my breast. He doesn't move.

When I was first in Venice, my then boyfriend and I were actors in a Tino Sehgal piece. Tino called us interpreters, called his work a constructed situation. We would invite another couple to dinner at a restaurant. When the first course started, Gianfranco would stand up and leave the table. Then, forty-five seconds later, I too would leave the table. We'd stay away for five minutes—one night making out in the bathroom, another night doing a crossword puzzle—and then return to sit at one another's places. I would finish Gianfranco's food; he would eat mine. When our guests asked what was going on, we'd simply say, "This is a work by Tino Sehgal entitled *Those Thoughts*."

Sometimes when I'm tired, I think I see Gianfranco inside a store or getting off a boat. I am about to call to him when I remember he's dead.

The February 2010 Chilean earthquake moved Earth's axis by about eight centimeters, thereby shortening the day by about 1.3 microseconds. The 2004 Sumatra earthquake shortened the day 6.8 microseconds.

I tell them I am leaving for Austria the next morning. My husband texted to say he wasn't feeling well, and I should grab a bite on my own before bed. Naturally, they ask me to join them for dinner.

"Let's play a game," Lori says as the waiter pours the third bottle of wine. "Do you know any games, Anita?"

I think strip poker; I think truth or dare. "I can't think of any," I say.

"Let's play, I never stole . . ." she says. "We each write down the biggest thing we've ever stolen and then we guess who wrote which one." I wonder what Lori has stolen in her life—a lipstick, a grapefruit, a kiss?

"I know your handwriting," Peter says.

"We'll dictate . . . to the waiter," Lori says.

I think of their hotel room. I think of all the things in it I could have taken home with me: light bulb, alarm clock, number from the door, and how I could have convinced myself I needed each one.

We take turns whispering to the waiter who writes different words on three different paper napkins, sets them face down on the table, and then disappears.

Lori shuffles the napkins and hands one to Peter who reads, "My mother's pain meds."

"You have to say, 'I never stole my mother's pain meds,'" Lori corrects him.

"But I did," Peter says.

"Peter!"

"It was only one, and she had plenty . . ." He is grinning, enjoying himself.

"You gave it away. Now we only have mine and Anita's left," Lori says. Her voice is calm. For the first time I wonder if I have underestimated her.

When I initially saw the two of them, inside the gallery—she looking at the prints on the wall, cocking her head, twirling the sweaty bits of hair at her neck around her pointer finger; he flipping through the catalog, lifting his head to look at what she pointed at, nodding, standing close to her in the heat—it was the gallery owner I most related to. He sat behind a small white desk, waiting. Knowing he had what they wanted.

For a few moments, no one says anything. The two unread napkins lie next to one another in the middle of the crumb-laden table.

"I'll guess which one is yours and which one is hers then," Peter says. "You can read the first one."

He hands his wife a napkin. The center of gravity seems to be shifting away from me as Lori reads, "I never stole a note from my husband's pocket."

Peter laughs instinctively and fumbles in his empty pocket. He knows there is a game going on and he knows he is no longer playing.

"Give her the other one," Lori says, staring straight at me. Peter picks up the final paper and hands it to me with a weak smile.

Lori prompts, "You never stole . . ."

I try to think of all the things I ever stole and what it would be like to say aloud that I never stole them. What that would do.

I think, *I never stole what you didn't want me to have.* I think how a confession so quickly turns to an attack. Then I think of all the double negatives that become positive: not uninteresting, not unclaimed, not unfeeling.

"You never stole," Lori repeats. And now it sounds like perhaps I never did. Perhaps Lori gave me Peter and per-haps Peter gave me a child and perhaps I gave them to one another anew. Perhaps we each got what we came for.

I crumple the napkin, stuff it in my still-full water glass, and say, "Anything that mattered."

Tiny House

SHE RENTED THE TINY house online. It looked perfect—deep-blue cabinets, toe-kick drawers, window wall, farmhouse sink . . . but when she arrived, she could not find it. As the rental agreement stated, the key was located under the large rock by the twin-trunked tree at the end of the lane. The landscape was exactly as described—a meadow of larkspur and goldenrod. The day was mild, and there was a light breeze. Everything was just so, except the tiny house. It wasn't there. Perhaps, she thought, giddily, it was tinier than she'd supposed. Suppose it was so tiny she'd stepped right over it. Or on it! What if she'd crushed the

tiny house? But that was ridiculous. She held the key in
her hand, and it was a key like any other house key, if a
little smoother, a little brighter. A key made of moonlight
or mother-of-pearl.

Check-in, the email said, was not possible before 4
p.m. She'd pushed it. Arrived at 3:45 thinking it was close
enough, but the tiny house was not there. Might it appear
in the meadow at 4 p.m. promptly? That must be it, she rea-
soned. The cleaners might have a special tiny house cleaning compound where they rolled the houses in and then
rolled them back out sparkling, like a car from a car wash.
She decided to wait. But what if they did not want her to
see them rolling in the tiny house? It might be inappro-
priate. Like sitting outside a hotel room while the housekeeper made the bed after someone else had slept in it.

She needed to find the tiny house, but first she needed
to raise her blood sugar. She had not eaten since breakfast some nine hours earlier. She opened her backpack
(everything she needed for the month was in her backpack, it was a tiny house, after all), and rummaged around,
hoping to find something to eat. Not even half an energy
bar left in a pocket.

Hungry and foodless, she got into her car, a rental also,
and backed out of the lane. She followed the road back
down a hill and along a marsh. Birds swooped overhead.
When the road forked, she went the way she had not come
and, after some turns, arrived in a very small town: post
office and town hall shared a low-slung building, and next

to it was a field with some tents where a few people milled and a clump of children chased one another; a leashed dog yapped at the scene, and a sign said, FARMERS' MARKET TODAY NOON – 4 P.M. She pulled into the nearly empty grass lot. The vendors were packing up their remaining items, but she bought a peanut butter oatmeal bar and a plum from one vendor. Another sold her half a cup of lemonade—all he had left, and from a third she bought, for a splurge and to counteract a creeping sense of absence, an extravagant bouquet of wildflowers.

To familiarize herself with the town, she continued in the direction she'd been going. Aside from what she'd already seen, though, there was only a real estate office and a package store. By the time she returned to the address on the email it was 4:30. As she pulled into the lane, she imagined the tiny house would be there, exactly as pictured on the website. It was the O'Keeffe print above the loft bed that had clinched the deal. The bright pink flowers rising like flames from the narrow vase, bursting upward. Her high school art teacher had introduced her to O'Keeffe. She'd gone on to art school because of the O'Keeffe quote her teacher had read the class one afternoon: "I want them to see it whether they want to or not." When she arrived, the tiny house was still not there.

"What do you mean it disappeared?" asked John, when she phoned him.

"In the picture it's here next to the tree in the meadow at the end of the lane, but I'm here and it's not."

"I'll call," he said.

"No, I'll call," she said, suddenly remembering this was why she'd rented the tiny house for the summer: to break from John. To liberate herself from her need of him. For everything. She'd become so dependent! It was embarrassing.

"Okay," he said. "But in the meantime, I could do some investigating. I'm sure I could find a place nearby with a spare room."

"No, no," she said. "It'll be fine. I probably have the wrong address. There's probably a whole bunch of meadows that look like this around here." But the key under the rock? And the twin-trunked tree?

The number for the rental company rang and rang and finally someone picked up.

"What was the name on the reservation?"

She repeated her name and waited.

Her heart beat hard in her chest, and it seemed forever before the voice on the other end said, "Oh, yes. The Tiny House. What's the problem? No key?"

She told the woman again that no, she had found the key, it was just that the house wasn't there. There was a pause on the other end of the line during which she wondered if the woman thought she was an idiot. Or insane. Then, "I'll see what I can do." And the line went dead.

Had she given the woman her phone number? Yes, she had, with her name. Had the woman written it down? Probably she hadn't needed to; it would have shown on her end. She'll get to the bottom of it—call the cleaning company, have them roll in the tiny house right away. Yes, she was glad she'd thought of that. It was *an elegant solution to an inscrutable problem*. That's what John would say. John and his elegant solutions. She'd married him for them. Then separated for his inscrutable problems.

Insects sang. Clouds spread taffy-like across the sky. She sat on the hood of the car eating the peanut butter oatmeal bar, which proved surprisingly filling. Chipmunks chased one another up and around the twin-trunked tree and as she followed their spiraling trails with her eyes, she noticed a business card thumb-tacked to its bark. She hopped off the car and stepped forward onto one of the tree's great roots to read it, certain it was the missing clue to the whereabouts of the tiny house.

Dear Friend,

I am not here. I am neither gone nor disappeared nor snatched. I am not here because I want to be NOT HERE. This card is not intended as part of an extended tease, game, nor encouragement for investigation. Neither is this a metaphor. Thank you for respecting my decision. I regret any discomfort my absence may cause you.

It was not signed, but it did not have to be. It was, clearly, from the tiny house. She'd felt a kinship with it immediately, known this house was not like any other house in the world. And this proved it. Briefly she was filled with a deep satisfaction that her instinctive attraction to the tiny house, her powerful feeling of the specific personhood of it had been validated. She had a way of connecting like this. This is what had brought John into her life. She'd felt their kinship immediately, the moment she'd entered his Studio Art class freshman year, so when he had ignored her the entire first semester she had not despaired. She'd known, as one knows one day they'll die, that one day he'd turn to her, see her, want her, become her life. It was the same with the tiny house. So, it not being here changed nothing. She'd always known that gone was not actually an adjective but a noun. That it watched or waited or clung.

As an artist, she specialized in double-exposed self-portraits at once dreamy and uncanny—waving from a window of a barn inside a jar; veiled in barbed wire; standing in her kitchen disappearing into fog; two of herselves attached at the ribs, like the original Siamese twins; a staircase spiraling in her chest.

If you rent a tiny house that is not here, does that make the place where it is not tinier or huge, a space without end? John was also not here but he was elsewhere and though she'd called him, thought of him first, he was less here than the tiny house. Why was that? Because the tiny house, unlike John, in its not-here-ness was even more perfect.

Dear Tiny House,
    You have left me twice—first age five, the dollhouse

that never came. I know that was you, in your infancy. Have you grown? I have. Waiting. The second is now. This meadow is a beautiful place to be left. I'll watch for you up and down the day, every hour on the half-hour. I will not let you go, because you are mine. I hear you in the cicadas. Crepitations, stridulations, the clicks and flicks of your absence court me. I am here, at the foot of the twin-trunked tree, waiting like a worm for a bird, to be limp in your beak, unbroken. If I pulled out your hidden bed, flipped back your covers, slipped my feet between your sheets, would you be disappointed because you had known the shape of made, or do you aspire toward untucked, a life inhabited? Teach me. I remember everything-in-its-place but cannot find it. Have I mentioned I'm gluten-free and vegan now? The more I drop from my diet the farther I can see. Soon I'll be able to see you too. I have all these thoughts I cannot handle. You have the under-the-floor drawer they beg for. Who is to leave here first? Myself or my desire for you? What a privilege it is to be so desiring. How can a house so tiny loom so large?

It was a bit . . . breathless. Still, the emotions were true. She ripped her letter into ribbons and scattered them around the twin-trunked tree, circling it seven times, as in a Jewish wedding, calling forth her tiny home, their life together.

Time passed and the day deepened. She paced the meadow, chanting songs from her childhood, appealing to the mysterious humanity of the tiny house. She knew by heart its inventory. As if undressing for the first time before a beloved, she wrote an accounting of her own and tacked it to the tree where the business card had hung: seven single socks; three fillings, one crown; sunflower ankle tattoo; mesh lace garter corset, too large; two secret family recipes—strawberry pretzel salad, brown sugar beans; insomnia; blue-yellow color blindness; four nieces; two art degrees; one important photography monograph in the works; thirteen years of shooting weddings and b'nai mitzvahs; a basket of feelings; twenty-two years of successful birth control; several questions she'd like to ask dead relatives; a dream in which she eats Walter Gropius; debts to two strangers; a smoking habit, kicked; no allergies/no fetishes/no pets; one small scar from a childhood shovel fight; a spider bite on her thigh, still swollen; oversized prescription sunglasses, scratched; PMS, TMJ, IUD; $453.

She stepped backward. She searched for signs. Perhaps the tiny house had left some essence of itself in the ground, imprinted its spirit on the site. She found what she was certain were its footprints. Like the negative of a photograph or the impression left after a bright light on a TV screen, the ground shimmered with the outline of the tiny house, but only if she looked away.

She could feel it attracting her corporeality to its absence.

She lay on her stomach in the spot she was sure the tiny house had been and crawled over the grass to confirm its edges. Temperature shifts and a slight hum in her bones directed her navigations. Her phone vibrated. A text from John.

All set?

She thought for a moment, then sent a prayer hands emoji. She often used that one when communicating with her ex, because it was ambiguous: Thank you/Please/I hope/High five/Namaste. Let him think what he wanted; he would anyway.

He responded with a thumbs-up.

Then the phone rang. It was the woman at the rental.

"Apologies for the delay," she said. "Our fax was down. I did some workarounds though, backchecking, digging, bird-dogging . . ." There was the sound in the background of papers being shuffled and someone coughing. "Good choice, by the way. The Tiny House. Love that one." She cleared her throat. "First thing I want to say is I am not worried." A hawk circled overhead. "You have what I would say are a few options. You could wait and see. You could go away and come back. You could file a report. You could petition for a transfer. Or, you could consult with a specialist to put your mind at rest."

Her mind was perfectly rested, she said, a little offended.

"Terrific!" said the woman on the other end of the line. "Would you mind staying on after I hang up for a short survey?"

"No," she said. She meant no, do not hang up, but she heard the click, followed by an automated voice.

"On a scale of one to nine where one is highly agree and nine is highly disagree, please say or press the number that corresponds to the following:

My problem has been resolved.

My insurance covers this problem.

My problem is only a problem when viewed from a certain angle.

My problem is a gift from the universe sent to remind me that life is suffering, and suffering is to be accepted.

My ex got me into this problem, and he will get me out of it.

My problem is my own.

My problem is deep-rooted and complex.

The problem with my problem is that I do not know how long it will persist rather than that it inflicts actual pain upon me.

The problem with my problem is that I have no one to talk to about it.

My problem is hilarious.

I am embarrassed of my problem.

My problem is that I couldn't say when embarrassed *of* became common usage and it worsens my embarrassment . . ."

She hung up.

The moon, only a day old and barely visible, hung its thin crescent above her. Then the sudden loud screech of the hawk. Her focus sharpened and compressed.

Immediately, something felt different: Her body was simultaneously tucked in and spacious, and her center of gravity shifted—a deeper register, a higher view. The wind brushed her skin in a straight line, as if she met it smooth and flat.

When, exactly, did she realize she was changing?

The setting sun hit her eyes, and its gleam both reflected outward and penetrated into the space behind her pupils. A warm pleasure glowed inside her, and with it came a great anchoring like a boulder left by a receding glacier. The wildflowers she'd bought at the farmers' market rested close against her, an English front garden. She sat on the site where the tiny house had been . . . was becoming . . . would be again . . . creaking and groaning, settling.

HAPPY BIRTHDAY

THE MORNING HER HUSBAND left was also her fifty-first birthday. She opened the front door to find empty recycle bins strewn up and down the block, but in front of her house, boxes were neatly nested inside boxes beside the blue bin full of metal, glass, and plastic. Had she parked too close to the recycle, concealing it from the road? Nope. They'd just skipped hers.

Whatever. The day must go on. She brought her husband's six shirts to the dry cleaner. They were in her car; it was on the way; it's not like she'd need to pick them up again. At the dry cleaner, the guy with the face did not acknowledge her until she rang the bell on the counter even though he was standing right there.

Then, with a jump, and flustered, "Phone number?" He didn't meet her eyes but stared disconcertedly over her shoulder. Like he didn't know her. Like she hadn't small-talked him for years, commenting on the extreme heat, the coyotes, the spring snow, all the while diplomatically ignoring the skin-like-melted-wax on his cheek and neck. As if he hadn't long ago memorized the phone number on her account. As if he didn't recognize the model and make of her car, so that when she pulled up to the spot in front of the door, in front of where he stood all day, he would turn to the conveyor rack behind him to bring out her hus-band's suits or shirts or slacks, so that by the time she stepped up to the counter, whatever she'd come for hung on the bar sans the objectionable plastic sleeve as per the standing instructions on her account.

Perhaps he was only pretending not to know her, she thought as she drove away, because he sensed that she did not care to know him, i.e., thought of him, if at all, as the guy with the face.

Well, at least she *saw* his face. Last week she'd been relaxing with a cup of tea at the kitchen table after apply-ing the skin-softening kelp face mask, when her husband had walked right past her to scream up the stairs that she'd better come down, because the kitchen smelled like a beached whale carcass.

"I'm right here," she'd said, face covered in seaweed.

And he'd jumped, "What the hell!" It wasn't clear if he meant her sushi face or the sinister portal through which she must have magicked herself beside him.

How many times in the past year had her husband stood up suddenly into her chin and gotten a bloody nose, bumped a hand into her teeth and cut his finger, knocked an elbow into her jaw and hit his funny bone. "When did you become so sneaky?" he'd complain, nursing his latest wound. Transcending his inability to see her with his inability to see his inability to see her.

At the intersection ahead, a crossing guard stepped into the road with her handheld stop sign and then quickly jumped back as an oncoming car nearly hit her. Its driver was neither texting nor eating, nor did he seem to have noticed that he'd nearly killed the woman.

"I can't take it anymore," her husband had said, wiping blood from his forehead after he tripped over her feet and hit his head on the coffee table. "The way you creep up on me!" She'd been sitting on the couch reading all morning. They'd agreed to separate. Would sort out the details after telling the children. Who were in college. Who would not be surprised.

She walked into the yoga studio.

"Hi John," said the young woman at the desk to the young man who walked in just behind her. At the end of class, during Savasana, the teacher went around the room pressing shoulders and giving short head massages to everyone but her. Was she sweating too profusely or had the teacher simply not seen her? The last time her husband had rolled on top of her in bed, he'd jumped up screaming, "When did you get home?"

"It's so liberating!" Rachel said. They were lunching at the overpriced organic café halfway between the yoga studio and Rachel's office. "Not to be an object anymore. You can stare. The unobserved observer." Rachel leaned in. "Or steal," and she slipped a jar of jam off the table into her purse. It was all a gleaming reboot on the other side of menopause, according to Rachel. And not having a husband wouldn't change a thing, because, her friend confided happily, who had sex with their husbands anymore anyway?

It was her birthday, and her husband's gift to her was to leave her, which, truth be told, maybe wasn't the worst gift after all. But what about the birthday coupons? Wasn't her email inbox supposed to light up with birthday specials to spas and coffee shops and makeup chains? Had she really unsubscribed to *all* of them?

"We're all over," Rachel said, triumphant and plump. "Look around." And she was right! The café had looked empty when she'd first come in, but now that she looked around, the place was filled—table after table of women who, when the sun glinted off the tabletops, or they leaned against the back of the booth, were camouflaged. Stealth. Even if they weren't pale-skinned, they were faded, chalky, and their hair—so many shades of nothing—bled into the background of wherever they sat or stood, so you could practically walk right into one of them and not realize she was there except for a vague, mineral whiff.

A year ago, her husband had said he would stay for the kids. Now she thought he'd probably stayed because who leaves what isn't there in the first place?

When she got home, she sat down at her desk to write but couldn't concentrate. Yoga was supposed to help with this. So was being treated to a birthday lunch by a longtime friend. Instead, the computer blinked at her as if to say, What do I care if you never finish this story? It's about a middle-aged woman. I could give a fuck. Yawn.

The doorbell rang. When she got to the door, there was only the postcard: "Sorry we missed you. Please pick up your package at the post office on _____." He hadn't even bothered to write in a date.

"Hey!" she called, but the letter carrier was too far down the road to hear. Or else he was ignoring her, because better if she just came to the post office to pick up her vaginal moisturizer, and he didn't have to get her signature for it.

That's when it hit her. She got in her car and went to the station. The train to the city was just pulling in. She got on. No ticket. She sat down. Sure enough, no conductor bothered her. At Grand Central she walked between the tourists and commuters right to the head of the long, tired line at Starbucks. No one said a thing.

"Grande soy latte," she said to the pimply teen behind the cash register who seemed startled by her voice.

Someone looked up from his phone, about to object to her cutting the line, but then he noticed the two young women in front of him, and the moment passed.

As she walked through the station sipping her coffee, her husband called. He was at the restaurant, where was she? The kids were already there, and he thought they'd agreed to do this one last thing together. What should he tell them? She sighed and the call cut out.

The night was cool, and she could feel the heat of the day releasing like a long exhalation from the walls of the buildings. She wandered through the city streets, glancing at window displays, listening to fragments of other people's lives. When she got hungry, she followed the odor of garlic to a small pizzeria. Inside, was a single table where a single man sat, eating. He was either a creep or a decent human being. She had zero interest in finding out.

When her order was ready, she carried it to the table. With a swish of her arm, she pushed the man's tray onto the floor and replaced it with hers. He jumped up, furious. She watched as he quickly took her in—gray roots to bunions—and his anger melted to embarrassment.

She pulled his jacket off the back of the chair. "I think you left this," she said handing it to him as she took his seat.

DEEP HOLLOW CLOSE

THE WRITER LIVED ON Deep Hollow Close. There were only four houses. As the name of the street said, they were close. So close, the Writer's husband was fucking the next-door neighbor. The Writer had just discovered this fact in the form of a ruby stud earring caught in the upholstery of the back seat of his car. Her ears were unpierced. It was one of the things her husband implied he loved about her—not that she hadn't pierced her ears per se, but that she was "timeless." He said if someone saw a photograph of the Writer, they'd be unable to say in which century she lived. "My archetype" he called her.

The lease was up, and the Writer had cleaned out the car to return it. She'd found two rolls of dimes her daughter had collected. She'd found her mother-in-law's umbrella; her daughter's lip balm; a nose hair trimmer she'd bought her husband as a passive-aggressive gift that he'd never opened; a hardened, half-eaten protein bar; and this ruby earring.

You may think the Writer was jumping to conclusions. You may think a ruby earring that was not the Writer's could belong to: 1) her daughter, 2) a colleague of her husband's, 3) the wife of a couple friend of theirs, 4) a friend of her daughter's. You would be wrong because: 1) her daughter also did not have pierced ears, although she had just pierced her nose according to a text she'd recently sent the Writer from abroad, 2) the only colleague her husband had had occasion to drive anywhere was his business partner—a not-so-hip man who would not wear an earring and would also have had no need to sit in the back seat, 3) the only time they shared a car with couple friends was when they drove to dinner with Lori and Peter, because the parking at their favorite restaurant was a nightmare, and they always took the Browns' car since Lori was allergic to dogs and wouldn't risk the Writer's or her husband's cars even though Borges had been dead for five months, and 4) the last time her husband had driven any of her daughter's friends anywhere was before she had her license, in the days of the previously leased vehicle.

The ruby stud clearly belonged to the woman next

door, whose wardrobe consisted entirely of blacks and whites, accessorized in red—scarf, belt, hat, flats, ear-rings—startling bits of alarm glinting off her otherwise plain self.

The Writer had thrown out the half-eaten protein bar, donated the trimmer to her housekeeper's church sale, pocketed the lip balm, redeemed the dimes, returned the car, and was sitting in the backyard under her mother-in-law's umbrella, which made a perfect parasol. She was writing the next-door neighbor a note. Despite, or perhaps as a result of being a writer, the Writer rarely wrote. She was suffering a dry spell. Day after day the Writer walked, read, listened to podcasts . . . hoping for the spark that would reignite her imagination, but for months now she had written nothing. To ceremonialize the occasion that had brought her pen back to paper, the Writer was writ-ing with a purple fine-point Sharpie on a piece of birch bark, twirling the ruby earring between her left thumb and forefinger. The end of the stud was sharp and pricked her finger, drawing blood.

Dear Amy,

Your ruby earring wedged in the seat of my car means one of two things: Either you're fucking my hus-band or you used to fuck my husband. In either case, if you have overheard my husband call me timeless and are raising an eyebrow over my use here of the f-word, rest assured, it does not date me. According to

Melissa Mohr, author of *Holy Sh*t: A Brief History of Swearing,* fuck appears to have hit its stride by the late sixteenth century. Incidentally, did you hear about the summa cum laude cake ordered by the proud mother of a high school graduate that arrived with its middle word missing because some supermarket employee flagged it for profanity? Cum on! That is to say, I am going to make your life here on Deep Hollow Close as fucking deep and hollow and close as I can.

What to do next? The Writer felt instantly better, having just made a terrific threat, but quickly not so good again, as she had no idea how to live up to this threat. What the Writer did when she felt lost: etymology. The damp cave of history, its readable beasts.

She was, according to her phone (where would the Writer be without untrammeled access to the information superhighway?), a cuckquean: Middle English, 1562, female equivalent of a cuckold. It was nice to have a name. It was nice to have a provenance.

The Writer noted with interest the derivation of cuckold: the cuckoo's habit of laying its eggs in the nests of other birds. The cuckoo pushes one egg from the host's nest, lays her own, and flies away. A memory came to the Writer: arriving with her toddler daughter at another woman's house for a playdate, claiming an urgent errand, and driving home to write for the next hour, alone. One's "it takes a village" is another's brood parasitism.

The Writer sucked the blood from her finger and with the other hand scrolled. While the cuckold is a fool, the cuckquean is a fetishist—aware of, encouraging, and enjoying her husband's affairs. The Writer's face flushed. Was she aware of? She'd noted a recent self-consciousness in her husband regarding the neighbor. He seemed to stand straighter when he got into his car if she was outside. Suddenly conscious of his posture. And last week, when she'd commented on Amy's legendary rudeness: "I drove right by her, waving, and she didn't so much as smile back."

"Maybe she didn't see you," he'd said.

Of course, she'd seen her. "She needs a boyfriend," the Writer had blurted. "She'd be friendlier if she got laid."

"That's a pretty sexist thing to say, isn't it?" her husband had said. But hadn't he blushed a little too?

And had she encouraged? Last month she'd sent her husband next door to convince Amy to cut down the cedar that threatened to fall on their porch. How long had he been over there? What had he mumbled when he returned? "She'll get back to me"? The cedar's branches waved threateningly above the Writer's head even now.

Humiliation of the cuckquean, the Writer read, may be intentional, accidental, or incidental. Aside from the paradoxical pleasure afforded by the justifiable excuse to sit alone in her yard with the hastening of her own heartbeat, the only real enjoyment the Writer would ever derive from her cuckqueaning would be through the poetic justice of a fairy tale, her favorite genre—blood-soup and gold. Under her fake online name, Dory-Anne Graying, the Writer posed a question to the hive mind: Favorite fairy tales about adultery?

Soon the Writer was lost in a sea of message boards about fairy tales with adultery themes, where tale after tale was told from the point of view of the cuckold and not one from the perspective of a cuckquean. Gamely she persisted in her research, certain she'd find some once upon a time with the outline of a plan.

In "Husband's Revenge," a man paid back his friend's trespass by fucking his wife. Reciprocation had its appeal. The next-door neighbor's husband, though, was dead. Perhaps her son—one of those broad-shouldered man-boys who ranged the suburbs profiting from and oblivious to their cinematic privilege. Seducing a high school boy was briefly an attractive idea, but when she imagined a six-teen-year-old's aptitude for sex, she recognized the scale of the fantasy-reality gap. Plus, the boy was mostly away at his prep school, rumored to be paid for by Firestone after the tire of his father's SUV flew off on the parkway, sending him to his death as he drove home from work.

Next the Writer discovered the original Italian Sleeping Beauty where Beauty was awakened by birthing the twins of an adulterous rapist. The Writer was appalled— childbirth forced on a comatose victim, children fed to their father, aggrieved wife burned alive—and enthralled. Was she the evil wife? Would she sacrifice her offspring to punish her cheating husband? Into the incompleteness of Beauty, she poured what she knew of the neighbor, bread-crumbing her way to a shared experience. This was the problem with stories. They bred empathy.

The sound of motors roused the Writer from her online investigation. She walked to the edge of the yard from where she could see a squadron of men swarming the neighbor's lawn with weed whackers, blowers and mowers. On the side of their truck: EDEN LANDSCAPES, WE'RE GREAT IN BEDS.

The Writer walked around the house, down the driveway and across the street. She stopped at the four mailboxes, gathered the bills and ads from her own, and slipped the birch-bark message into the neighbor's.

The Writer began watching the next-door neighbor. Early mornings Amy jogged. The Writer caught her leaving and returning. She looked defiant when she jogged—each step a little struggle, her arms—skinny but muscled—forming pump fisted right angles at her sides. Both women had earbuds in their ears. The Writer imagined Amy was listening to some pop song fitness playlist. In her own ears was a podcast on morality:

Scenario one. Five workers are working on a train track and unbeknownst to them, a train is barreling toward them. They are too far to warn. You are next to a lever which, if you pull, will make the train jump the track and instead of killing the five workers, it will hit one single worker working on another track. Will you pull the lever? If you say yes, you are with nine out of ten. The Writer watched Amy approach her driveway, absorbing the necessary choice.

The Writer could almost hear Amy's beachy beat music scoring her podcast.

Scenario Two. You are now on a bridge overlooking the tracks where the five doomed workers are working. They still cannot hear you calling out the danger, but on the bridge next to you is one stout man. If you push this one man onto the tracks, his body will stop the train and save the five workers. Do you push the man? It was still the same math—sacrifice one to save five.

Amy slowed her jog, neared her door, and then stopped, hands on her knees, panting. If the man were her husband, the Writer would push him. When the Writer pictured putting her hands on her husband's back and shoving him over the low rail onto the tracks in front of the squealing train, she pictured Amy watching.

Amy turned toward the Writer. The Writer ducked behind the curtain, but just before she'd seen a small, hard smile crack her neighbor's face.

For days the Writer kept up a front. She planted pansies around the house. First in the flower box at the side door from where she could see into Amy's den.

The Writer had just read a study in which University of Chicago psychologists demonstrate that using a

foreign language made people less emotional and therefore more likely to overcome aversion to breaking taboos.
This would explain her neighbor's willingness to fuck the
Writer's husband. Henceforth, the Writer would think of
the next-door neighbor as French: Aimée. Plus, it was evi-
dently she who was loved.

Aimée's TV was always on, though the room remained
mostly unoccupied. Conclusion: Aimée needed the sound
of voices; she was not good at being alone.

When the Writer got around to the window box
by the front door, there it was: a small rectangular box.
The Writer and her husband rarely used the front door.
Typically, deliveries came to the side door, but when the
FedEx driver was on vacation or UPS changed the regular
driver's route, their subs occasionally left packages at the
front door where they sat, sometimes for days, before she
or her husband noticed them.

This one was addressed to her, and the cardboard
was sun-faded and badly warped. It had been soaked and
dried more than once. Box of rain, the Writer thought.
The return address on the wrinkled cardboard box was
smeared but appeared to be the same as the "send to"
address. That is, theirs. They shared the same address
as their three neighbors. Deep Hollow Close was once
owned by one family—main house, the Writer's; carriage
house, Aimée's; barn, Irish family's; caretaker's, Italian
couple's. She sat on the stoop a little (irrationally?) afraid
to open it. Why would one of her neighbors mail a box to

her when they could walk it over? Perhaps it was not from one of the neighbors; perhaps it was something dangerous that someone wanted there to be no way to return or trace, so they'd written the same address for addresser as addressee. Was this legal?

The Writer searched it on her phone, which was, as always, in her back pocket. It was not illegal to duplicate the return and send to address, so long as adequate postage was provided. Could it be drugs? The Writer was known to enjoy the occasional edible. If so, she might partake before sharing it with her husband. Perhaps they could reconnect over a stoned dinner for two on the back patio: He'd confess; she'd forgive, and that would be that until sobriety kicked in, along with her building dissatisfaction over her life as literary up-and-comer turned wife and mother.

The Writer opened the box. Every bad decision had at least the potential to be material. Inside: a hand-sized ceramic sculpture of Mother Theresa in a red bikini entitled, *The Ideal Wife*. Shaken, the Writer quickly resealed it, went inside, and hid it in the back of her closet. She'd sculpted it herself. Years ago. Before she was married.

Previous to the Writer being a writer, she'd played at being an artist. Her mother, who admired sculpture, had taught her about negative space. At the time, the Writer had been reading Freud and was obsessed with the Madonna-whore complex. By then, she'd successfully auditioned for both parts: Her first boyfriend wanted to marry her but kept putting off "making love." Her next fucked her in public parks but wouldn't acknowledge her around his friends. The Writer had last seen *The Ideal Wife* in the studio she'd shared with two other artists. They'd had the space barely six months when the landlord had locked them out for unpaid rent. She'd forgotten all about that.

Could the appearance of the sculpture have something to do with Aimée? Somehow, everything strange and wrong should lead to Aimée. Why was the Writer focused on the neighbor and not her husband? This was not a feminist response to betrayal! Assuming the man was just a pawn of the women. Or was it? Assuming the women had the real power. Did the Writer care less about her husband than she did about her own ego, which had been deeply wounded by another woman taking what was rightfully hers? Whose? The other woman's or the Writer's? Rightfully the Writer had to admit she and her husband had not been great lately. She had, in fact, been pretty angry at her husband for some time now. For what? Everything and nothing—his nose hair, his smell, the time he forgot to flush the toilet before work and his shit sat in the bowl under the lid for eight hours before she discovered it. For not making her feel brilliant and important and gorgeous like he used to. For making more money than she did. For making her rely on his money. For having a doctorate when it was she who ought to be the doctor in the family—Doctor of what? Resentment? For not being a woman, for making the Writer wish her husband were a woman when she herself was not even a lesbian; for the parts of him that were male. Not the genitals, which were fine, but the assumptions and opinions which were certain and oversimplified and unexamined and sometimes right. Especially when he was right. That really galled her. So, when the Writer realized her husband was fucking the next-door neighbor, a part of her felt this was right. As in, to be expected. Predictable. And as such, less interesting. Than what? Than the woman who wanted to fuck him?

The Writer was many things: hurt, lost, ashamed . . . but first she was a writer, and the responsibility of a writer was to her characters. The failure the Writer felt over the revelation that her husband was yet another disappointing character in a cliché narrative was mitigated by the discovery of a new character: Aimée, mysterious and compelling—a justifiable fixation. In all the Writer's stories, it was the women who were the most interesting. Recently, the Writer heard another writer say she wrote her book from the perspective of a man, because a man's perspective was the same as a woman's if a woman could do whatever she wanted. The Writer wrote about women doing whatever they wanted. Who needed another man doing whatever he wanted? Her husband had gone and done what he wanted, and there was nothing new in it. Nothing singular or intriguing. But Aimée was another story. The woman next door could be anyone the Writer wanted her to be—a menace, a tease, a match. What did learning your husband was having sex with another woman do to a writer? Opened a storyline.

The next day Aimée came out to collect her empty recycle bin from the curb. The Writer was watching, and Aimée caught sight of her at the window. Aimée stared back at the Writer. No sign of alarm or remorse or shame. She held the blue bin in two hands and looked at the Writer as though she were gazing in a mirror.

The Writer waited until Aimée drove away and then slipped into her unlocked back door. She hadn't been in the house since two years earlier when she and her daughter brought over a plate of welcome brownies for the young widow and her son. The neighbor's boy had not been home, so her daughter had quickly left, and the two women had stood in the kitchen awkwardly.

"They're organic," the Writer had said, "and gluten-free."

"Are you a nutritionist?" Aimée had said.

"Oh no," said the Writer. "We just didn't know if you had any dietary restrictions."

"I don't eat sweets," Aimée had said. The Writer had laughed. Then quickly stopped because it was clear Aimée was not joking.

"Well, enjoy!" the Writer had finally said, after it was obvious Aimée was not going to invite her to stay.

Now the Writer went up the stairs. The first door opened to the master bedroom—antique iron bed, chaise by the window through which the Writer could see her

own house, and a carpet like a grass path leading to a
large walk-in closet. She stepped in. On the wall was a
sign: NO PHOTOGRAPHING, NO VIDEO RECORDING. The
Writer's eyes widened. Aimée and humor. The combination was news to her. The Writer's husband must like
this about her—discovering lightness where only gravity
was expected. The Writer took out her phone and photo-
graphed the sign. She took a short video of herself twirling on the rug in front of the sign. Breaking easy-to-break
rules came naturally to the Writer, who enjoyed jaywalk-
ing, wearing her shoes inside, bringing her own bever-
ages to movies.

She walked deep into the closet. She was not sure
exactly what she was looking for, but she'd know it when
she saw it. The Writer startled at the thought: pornogra-
phy with her husband and Aimée? Now she could not help
imagining them: she on top, of course, holding his arms
back. He with that stricken look he got when he knew he
was caught enjoying something he shouldn't—a third whis-
key, a sexist joke. Maybe that was why he'd been sleeping
with Aimée. She didn't hold him to higher standards.

The Writer fingered the clothes: black and white
slacks and blouses, lots of synthetic fabric. The Writer had
never bought anything she'd call either slacks or a blouse.
She tried on Aimée's shoes, though they were narrow. Tee-
tered in a pair of pimento-colored ankle-high heel boots
that made her calves look tight and hard. She wrapped
a scarlet scarf around her throat. It smelled of a woody

perfume. She ran her fingers over the closet's wood walls. Wormy chestnut.

Solitude, "a worm in the brain"—the line from an Edith Wharton story came to mind.

There was a thick closeness in this dark antique house. In these red shoes, it seemed to the Writer a not unthinkable thing to lend the still-young widow her husband. Was recruiting your husband's lover as your sex surrogate an antidote to the humiliation of being cuckqueaned? It must be the perfume working its way under her skin.

Suddenly the Writer had the strangest sense she was being observed. She told herself she was projecting. That it was the signs about the filming and photographing. But it was not a mechanical watcher she felt. It was like eyes. On her.

She pushed her way into Aimée's hangers like a child in a department store hoping to hide beneath the racks of clothes, and that's when she found the door. Waist-high and handle-less. When she pressed on it, she heard a latch release, and it swung inward. The Writer was afraid, and she was curious. Afraid of whomever or whatever had been watching her in the closet. She no longer felt its eyes on her. And curious about what Aimée hid in a closet behind her closet. As if in answer to any last hesitation, a surprisingly fresh odor issued from the small doorway, and the Writer crawled in.

She expected darkness but was met instead with daylight. Looking up, the Writer saw a small window in a gable, propped slightly open. Over the entire floor, storage bins were stacked. Towers of brown boxes with clear front panels like tree trunks with eyes. Between the dark brown towers, paths branched in every direction. Cold air eddied around her ankles. One by one, the boxes turned their eyes to her. She assumed the chill she felt was from the open window.

When she peered into the clear front panels of the boxes, she recognized everything inside them: The mohair unicorn she'd gotten for her sixth birthday with its yellow matted horn; her seventh-grade math textbook; five issues of *Love Diary,* the comic she'd devoured as a kid; a paper target sheet with its perfect concentric circles and a hole ripped just left of its center; a signed CD she'd never played called *Ari's Arias*, given to her by the operatic girlfriend of the man upstairs when they'd still lived in the city. . . . The Writer's days archived in lost things, down to the taxidermied body of their runaway rabbit. She was shivering. Just then she heard a car.

She knew she should leave—run, tell her husband, go to the police . . . but she didn't. As if pushed by a gust, she moved deeper into the space, trailing her hand over the boxes, which she now noticed were each numbered. In one, labeled 1000.04, she found her Red Door Sweet Shop apron from when she'd worked at the bakery as a teen. Beneath it was a box numbered 00375 containing a well-loved copy *If on a Winter's Night a Traveler.* She'd completely forgotten about the book. The Writer was queasy, overcome with the sense of her own porousness, as if she'd stumbled into the prop room of a peek-a-boo theater only to discover that what had been disappeared was her own self.

She pressed palms against eye sockets, then dropped hands at her sides, and looked again. The forest of boxes seemed only to have grown. In 159.9558 she found a dozen packets of Hershey's Kissables—her daughter's favorite childhood candy, discontinued. She turned and her foot knocked the top off a smaller box marked 306.722 filled with assorted jewelry. She pulled out a bracelet— macramé and turquoise—her husband had bought her on their first trip together, before they'd married. She'd lost it one day at the beach years later. She heard Aimée outside closing her car door, opening and closing her trunk, opening and closing her back door, dropping something on her kitchen counter which, the Writer realized, was directly below her.

The Writer concentrated on the cool air going in through her nostrils and the warm air going out. She slipped out of the red shoes and quietly padded between the towering stacks in search of the first box, but the numbers, some as many as eight digits long, obeyed no design that she could fathom. From outside she heard the rapid drumming of a woodpecker and the insistent bark of a dog. She found 1.0000009 and inside it was the wool beanie the Writer had worn on their last house-hunting excursion twenty years ago. She'd been sure she'd left it in the real estate agent's car, but when the woman had checked her back seat, it wasn't there.

She didn't know how long she sifted among the thicket of boxes, lifting tops and fingering their contents, reviewing lost frames of her life as if it were a film to be unspooled. Soon, however, darkness fell, and the Writer could hear Aimée's voice issuing from the den. The Writer froze, afraid she'd been caught, but it was not the tone of accusation. The Writer realized with relief that Aimée was on the phone. She realized, too, that this was her chance to leave.

As the Writer stepped out of the secret room and into the closet, she noticed a poster on the wall she hadn't seen before. NOT YOUR HUSBAND'S BAND, it said in a punk rock font above a photograph of two pairs of women, guitars slung across their chests, squatting cheek to cheek. The Writer stepped closer. Actually, there were six of them— two of the women appeared half-hidden on the right side— artfully ripped stockings, spiked hair. The Writer tilted her head, squinted for a better look, and realized it was, in fact, only one woman, Aimée, with a guitar, crouching in a triangular space between two mirrors. She was mesmerizing. Aimée's voice was suddenly louder, and again the Writer froze. Aimée was coming up the stairs. The Writer huddled behind a black dress, her pulse pounding in her ears. Aimée was in the bedroom now. The Writer could see her red-painted toenails as she approached the closet.

"Yes, fine," Aimée said. She was close enough now that the Writer could hear the electronic on-hold tune playing from Aimée's phone. Just when the Writer was about to charge out of the closet and come at Aimée screaming (she would not be caught hiding), the bare feet turned, the tinny music receded, and the bathroom door clicked shut. The Writer sprang from the closet, raced down the stairs, slipped out of Aimée's back door and in through her own. Heart beating wildly, the Writer stared out her kitchen window at the house next door which was already calling her back.

Every day that week, the Writer returned. As soon as Aimée drove away in the morning, she ran between their houses, in the back door, up the stairs, across the bedroom, into the walk-in closet, and through the hidden door to the secret back room. She didn't want to go; she had to. Each time the chill. Each time the shock of the stacked storage boxes which seemed either to move around or to contain new items. The visits themselves seemed choreographed by the room itself. When she was in the room, time disappeared, and the Writer thrummed with a nervous energy she could almost call inspiration. Terrifying and exciting. As if under the influence of a powerful stimulant, her heart raced, her hands sweated, and the objects proffered ideas. She could see whole story arcs—her lavender eye pillow: Sleeping Beauty retold in the present from her own comatose point of view; baggie of her daughter's baby teeth: teacher touring a nuclear power plant with the fetus of her unborn twin growing inside her; the old hut-shaped salt and pepper shakers: woman becomes a tiny house. Flashes of subplots—an old lunar calendar: a women's immersive weekend retreat; her diaphragm: a pregnant bride. Thematic connections—her massage oil: desire; her carnival mask: impersonation. Motifs—stained smock: artists; her pocket mirror: doubles; an old fake ID: cons. She heard a haunting refrain, "*Go your own way.*"

When she returned home, she was starved, exhausted, unable to focus. The Writer tried to summon the clear energy she felt in Aimée's attic, but inside the walls of her own house, any ideas she could remember were either tiresome or impossible. Soon the Writer was counting the hours until she could wander the attic floor again probing the boxes—focused, engaged, immersed.

For the seventh visit, the Writer got an idea. She went to the back of her own closet and retrieved her old Nikon F3HP. She had not used it since her daughter was in middle school and miserable, and the Writer thought photography might help her find her way back to herself. They'd spent a cold afternoon in the woods as her daughter tested out the manual controls, and the Writer waxed rhapsodic about the shared language between photographer and subject and the reward of searching, seeing, being seen. As they'd developed the film in the basement darkroom—inherited from the previous homeowner, the Writer had told her daughter how Native Americans initially believed a photograph could steal a person's soul, then later saw photographs as links to the spirit world. The whole endeavor, however, had come to an abrupt end when the results were revealed to be a parade of accidental double exposures, and her daughter made it clear she'd never go down to the darkroom again. "It's just depressing," she'd said.

Now the Writer took the camera with her next door. Upstairs she removed it from its case and aimed it at the forest of boxes in what she now thought of as Aimée's Attic of Object Permanence. Her phone as always, was in her pocket. But she didn't want to take phone pictures. What the Writer wanted was historical, archival. Anxiety and hunger wrestled in her gut. As she peered through the eyepiece, she felt an inrush of calm. She pressed the shutter release. Click of capture, flush of joy. The Writer advanced the film, adjusted the focus, and began to prowl the floor. She no longer cared whether Aimée had fucked or was fucking her husband. Or rather, she was glad she had or was, because had she not suspected their affair, the Writer would never have found this treasure, which, like all treasures was charged and personal. She was after the souls of the objects. She wanted their texture, their character, their grain. A second before her eyes registered each photograph, she sensed its mood, subject, composition. The Writer circumambulated the room, framing it again and again. In the photographic flashes of the secret room, her life returned to her. When the camera would no longer advance, she rewound the film, opened the camera back, pocketed the film.

That night the Writer made turkey—tryptophan, served wine—melatonin, ended the meal with chamomile tea—apigenin, and when her husband finally headed up to bed, she took the roll of film from her pocket and quickly headed down the stairs. As soon as she reached the basement darkroom, she closed the door behind her and turned out the light. She was calm and focused. Safety glasses, gloves, developer, stop bath, fixer. It was soothing to follow a prescribed set of motions. This was why people like diets, she thought. And exorcisms.

The damp darkroom smelled of chemicals and fungus. The odor reminded the Writer of the article she'd read about an underground fungal network that connected different plants at their roots. What did they call it? The Wood Wide Web, she remembered as she rinsed the film reel, then soaked it in wetting agent. Like the plants that linked to the fungal network for information, nutrients, and sometimes sabotage, she and Aimée were linked.

The Writer took the film off the reel and unrolled it. Though the light was on again, she didn't look at the images yet; she would savor them later, after the film was dry and clean. She cut the film into strips and clipped them to the wire over the sink. Some plants engaged in petty theft through the fungal network, she remembered reading. The phantom orchid, she recalled, has no chlorophyll and steals its energy from neighboring trees. After placing a second clip at the bottom of each strip to keep it taut, the Writer went back upstairs to wait.

The Writer made herself another cup of tea and tried to settle on the couch. She was restless, though. She paced. She could burst from her body, race around the house as a pack of wolves. The point of the article, she remembered now: There was no such thing as an independent life.

Her husband snored upstairs as the moon rose above the trees. Back in the darkroom, the Writer checked that the films were dry, wiped away the few streaks with film cleaner, then finally held the first negative to the light.

What had happened to her photographs? The Writer was overcome with a sharp, guttural fear that made breathing hurt. She blinked, moved her face closer to the film. But the pictures were stunning, and quickly terror morphed into desire. They were close-ups of naked women's bodies—thighs on a chair; stomach against a sink; buttocks in a doorway; a torso on a mattress, legs spread—dusky human landscapes, lonely and panoramic, seen through a rain-spotted lens. Her hands grew hot as she held each image to the light. There was an intimacy about these photographs—searching, seeing, being seen— and a dare. Then it dawned on the Writer: Although her face was never shown, the subject in all of the frames was the same woman, and the rain-spotted lens was a window. These pictures were not posed but caught. And then, with a nauseating flush of adrenaline, the Writer saw between two raindrops, the mole, halfway down the thigh. The woman in the photographs was herself.

All night, the photographs burned behind the Writer's eyes. She saw them in every hypnagogic dream.

The next morning, the Writer awakened with a dark understanding and a sharp sense of purpose. Aimée was not a seductress or a thief. She was a curse. And a curse was broken by the instrument through which it was cast. The Writer dressed quickly. She retrieved the ruby stud earring from the drawer in her bedside table where she'd kept it and slipped it into her front pocket. As she walked down the stairs, the earring pressed into her hip, sticking her with every step.

In the kitchen her husband asked—it must have been the weekend, her husband had not gone to work—"Did you get the mail yesterday?" By which he meant, why didn't she?

"Must have forgotten," she said.

Out he went.

As if in perverse answer to her mounting sense of urgency, Aimée did not leave her house all day. Her husband returned, then left again. In the stillness of the wait, the Writer called to mind the items she'd found the day before:

In Box 407.22, the newspaper clipping, "New Mother Named One of Twenty Writers to Watch." Accompanying photo of the Writer at her desk: books lined up behind a coffee mug; her daughter in a baby rocker sleeping below. Her high school yearbook. The Writer's senior photo, bangs, big hair, and quote, "I don't do drugs. I am drugs."

—Salvador Dali. On the superlatives page, her name beside: "Most Likely to Spot a Ghost."

A car drove by on the main road, and the Writer heard the thump of a bass line from its radio, reminding her of the songwriter who sounded like God crooning a lullaby. She pulled up his greatest hits album on her computer and listened as she waited. Waiting and listening had always been her forte. She thought, as she gazed through the screened windowpane, that time and space were illusions, because although the songwriter was dead, he was here with her and although she was sitting at her kitchen table, she was roaming a room of lost objects.

Finally, long after the Writer's husband had returned and gone to bed, Aimée opened her back door. She was wearing a black suit with a red scarf over her head and was carrying a suitcase. The Writer's computer was streaming a radio story about two pairs of identical twins where one child from each pair was accidentally sent home with the wrong family. Aimée turned slightly, as if posing. "Twenty-five years after the switch, the truth is discovered," said the narrator. Aimée put down her suitcase. "They weren't who they thought they were." Aimée sucked in her stomach, tugged at the bottom of her suit jacket. "In short, everything about their life was a lie." Headlights appeared, followed by a car that pulled up to where Aimée was standing. "The scene where they first meet is captured on someone's phone." Aimée leaned in to say something to the

driver and, when the trunk popped open, tossed her suitcase in and slipped into the back seat. The Writer's hands
were tingling as she rose, stiff from her daylong vigil at the
kitchen table. "They steal glances at one another and shift
from side to side." As the car backed out of the driveway,
Aimée turned in the direction of the Writer and the two
women stared at one another. "They have stayed in touch.
They have a common email address. They really are very
close." The Writer blinked, and the car drove down to the
road, turned, and disappeared.

The Writer checked that her husband was asleep before
sneaking back downstairs and out the door. For a moment,
she was panicked. The door did not budge. Then, with
a small suction sound, it gave, and she was in. Was she
expected? There was a full glass of water on the counter.
And under the glass dome, sitting on the cake plate,
one thick slice of black forest. Her favorite. She took a
sip of the water. A cold emptiness ran down the back of
her throat, and though she'd spent the entire day in the
kitchen, she realized she hadn't eaten a thing since breakfast. The Writer pulled a knife from the knife block and
cut a thin sliver of cake, thinking Aimée wouldn't notice
if the slice was an eighth of an inch thinner. As soon as
the cherry whipped cream hit her tongue, she knew she
would eat the whole thing. Quickly, silently, she did. Then
she drained the water from the glass. Her mouth hummed
with a sugary metallic vibration.

She rinsed the knife, wiped it dry on a dish towel, and replaced it in the knife block. Then she washed the cake plate and glass and replaced them in the cupboard. It felt natural to be in this kitchen. Everything was located exactly where she expected it would be. The Writer felt a building excitement as the sugar hit her bloodstream.

She took the stairs two at time. Aimée's bed was made and on it was a note. The Writer was certain it was for her. Certain she'd been led to this moment like a fish to the hook. Still, she approached. Heart pounding, she lifted the paper off the bed. Just then, a car down the road backfired and the Writer jumped, dropping the note on the floor. She scolded herself for being so easily frightened, picked up the note and read: *What's Yours is Mine*. A wave of cold rushed through her, traveling up from her heels along her spine and into her head. She closed her eyes tightly and cradled her face in her palms.

When the Writer looked up, she saw the doors to the walk-in closet were open and there, just inside, sat a box like the boxes in the attic. Behind the box, the clothes had been pushed aside to reveal the inner door, which was, she now saw, open too. The clock by the bedside table, an old-fashioned alarm clock, ticked loudly. The Writer inhaled, counting, trying to slow her heartbeat. A diffusion of Aimée's perfume coated the insides of her nostrils making her momentarily dizzy.

When the room settled again, she approached the box. Neatly cataloged as 133.1133. The closer she got, the worse the smell. It was not, she realized, perfume. She was nauseated but unable to stop her feet from walking toward it. Against her better judgment, the Writer reached for the top, but the odor—Formaldehyde? Rot?—repelled her. Instead, she kicked it open. Slowly, she stepped close enough to look in.

Inside was a mass of what the Writer quickly realized was human tissue—a pear-shaped fleshy purse (Her gall bladder? Removed one month after her daughter was born), a pair of blood-covered masses like undeveloped, albino frogs (Her tonsils? Removed when she was five), and tucked into the corner, the Writer saw, just before she passed out, a three-inch long fetus, head half the size of its body, eyes fused shut (Her miscarriage).

She was struck in the face with the sun's rays. She was cold and her head hurt and at first, she did not know where she was. The bed was not familiar, the angle of the light was wrong. She flooded with panic. Then the panic slipped away, and she watched herself as if she were outside herself. She visualized her body from above as if she were a glacial erratic, stranded far from her original bedrock. Was she insane? Was someone inside her head? Watching her? If so, which her was her? She was the Writer! she remembered. And this was Aimée's bed. She did not remember climbing in but, judging from the light outside, she'd been there all night. She sat up quickly. There was a sharp pain at her hip crease. She reached into her pocket and pulled out the red earring. The clock on the bedside table showed 6:30. She had a half-hour before her husband woke.

Gripping the earring in her left hand, she headed for the secret closet. For a moment the Writer paused at the threshold of the walk-in closet, remembering something awful—what? She looked around, but everything was as it always was—the grass-green rug leading into the closet, the black and white clothes, the red shoes and scarves and belts and hats, the little door hidden at the back that she now pushed open.

Inside, the rush of air, the fear, then the clarity, as if she'd jumped into a cold lake. For a moment she felt happier than she'd ever felt. She saw what she needed immediately—atop a tower of boxes, a rag doll. Her old Raggedy Ann—red yarn hair, white eyelet pinafore, black shoes. The Writer walked up to the doll, pressed her face to it, inhaled. Candy and dust. She froze, suddenly enraged. Emotions saturated different sections of the attic like microclimates, and the Writer was a sponge. A high-pitched note rang in her ears as the Writer raised the ruby earring to the doll's face, and with a powerful swiftness, stabbed it in the eye. The doll fell to the ground, knocking the lid off the top box upon which it sat.

Inside the box was a watch. The Writer's. The one her in-laws had given her in honor of her engagement. The one she'd taken to the jeweler last week for a new battery, but never retrieved. She reached for it, and it was warm to the touch, as if it had just been taken off a wrist. The Writer's head hurt. The watch was ticking, but the date was wrong—not today's, but tomorrow's. She took the watch out of the box and fastened it around her wrist, testing the feel of the future.

"You're up early," her husband said from bed. She was standing in the doorway staring at him. His face was a story an old friend told about a place they'd visited that she could not remember.

Her husband rose, told her about the last-minute business trip he'd be leaving for that night.

"I'll be back by the weekend."

The image of Aimée standing outside with her suitcase flashed before the Writer's eyes.

She reached for her husband and pulled him toward her. His mouth was warm and stale from sleep. He stiffened with surprise. Then, recovering, tried to maneuver her to the bed, but she pulled him onto the floor. Soon her husband was on top of her; her hands were on his chest. Her legs were entwined behind his back; he could not move unless she let him. He stared at her. Slowly she circled her hips. He tried to move. Her legs tightened around him. He tried to speak. She put her tongue in his mouth, slipped it out, bit down on his lip. She held him there for hours, for days, for months, moving him through lifetimes where she was beneath him, on top of him, turned around, twisted, until he exhaled one last long loud time.

She had not come. She would finish after he left or when he was in the shower. Now, though, they lay side by side on the rug. Her skin glistened with sweat. Her heart pumped blood to every organ and back to itself.

"You should get going," she said. Her husband lingered for a moment, taking her in. He ran his fingers down the inside of her arm and into her hand. With a shiver, the Writer realized there was no watch on her wrist.

Slowly she turned to her reflection in the full-length mirror behind the bedroom door. There, in the white of her eye, was a fresh spot of blood.

The Time Museum

Some people treated their visit to the Time Museum as a holiday, others, as an obligation. I dressed up. Mascara-ed even my lower lashes and wore flared bell-bottoms because costume brought positivity to uncertainty; the pants were sequined. I admit I was a little nervous. People said it was like attending your own baby shower, but one in which a recording of your last breath played on a loop over the sound system. I could bring no one with me, because tickets to the Time Museum were strictly Admit One and arrived individually, even for couples who'd been together decades, even for twins.

The Time Museum was open all day every day of the year. Everyone got a ticket eventually. Everyone went. I was lucky. My ticket denoted an entrance on Friday at 2 p.m., so I only had to cancel a handful of patients. I suspected they were relieved.

Getting to the Time Museum was different for everyone; some people had to take an air balloon and then hike or board a ferry or ride a bike; no matter where in the world you lived, the Time Museum was accessible. This was one of the things that made it both inevitable and surprising.

For me, reaching the Time Museum required riding a monorail, followed by a cable car, and then a short walk. The museum sat on a hill just outside the city limits. Viewed from the city below, it appeared not to be there at all, though it cast a shadow. As I traveled, I looked for signs. An eagle flew by the window of the train, which I took to be auspicious; at the cable car station, a breeze lifted the hair from my shoulders and pulled a thick strand across my mouth, recalling the hair-sucking days of my girlhood before my mother cut it so short I had to assert my identity to all the adults around me. "I'm a girl!" I remembered correcting a secretary at the principal's office who'd thanked the "young man" delivering the attendance sheet. I do not miss those gendered days, though I do have a soft spot for all that forgotten paper—spelling lists, diaries with keys, snowflake chains, paper bag lunches with my name written in looping script.

Warned that the museum staff were sticklers, I sprinted the last quarter mile and arrived on time for my scheduled entrance. The Time Museum was a national landmark, and the guard at the gate was an aged man with a forelock, holding in one hand an hourglass and in the other a scythe. The walls of the entrance pavilion behind him were constructed of glass. It was the only museum entrance in the world from which a visitor could see sunset and moonrise simultaneously, a recorded greeting informed me as I stepped inside.

Once through the transparent reception, I followed the path through the arch that brought me into a gallery covered floor to ceiling in grandfather clocks. The ticking filled me with anticipation, as if the operational definition of time in action—that is, hundreds of repetitions of free-swinging pendulums—were deeply hopeful.

The museum featured an ever-changing selection of temporary exhibitions. On the day of my visit, in the first exhibit, sat a chair with an attached arm desk on which rested a ball of what looked like yellow playdough. I was invited to take a seat and play with the dough. The yellow substance was, I discovered after a dizzying few moments, Time Dough. That is, time made into a pliable physical substance to be manipulated into various shapes. The dislocations produced from my handling of the Time Dough resulted in torsions and curvatures that challenged my body's ability to strain and twist. After some nauseating molding in which I was flattened against the chair's back, pressed into the corner, and crushed into the seat of the chair desk, I rolled my portion of Time Dough into a snake and stability was reestablished.

Next, I put the two ends of the snake together and found myself seated in a circle of conjoined chair desks staring at myself all around me. Every time I moved an arm or shifted my weight or spoke, so did all the other me's, and like the elongated wooden chair desk on which we sat, we all seemed attached to one another, or rather to slip out of one another such that the towheaded child slid into the pimply teen who became the permed twenty-something who morphed into me pregnant, me middle-aged, me now, and me elderly in a continuous circle. At first, I felt physically ill. Soon, however, I discovered the trick was to allow the atoms of my body to glide and slip at low enough stress levels, hence the piped-in birdsong, to release the elastic energy needed to meet the curve's requirements.

The familiarity of the girls and women whose expressions ranged from curious to outraged to amused to knowing, made me feel deeply understood. "Hello," we said, nodding and smiling at one another over and over, and I was lost in that circular time-shape for I knew not how long, before a guard tapped me on the shoulder and asked me to roll the Time Dough back into a ball so the next visitor might have a chance with it.

Next, I found myself walking around a "rug" made of facts concerning time projected via lasers into a calligraphic tapestry on the floor. I paced the perimeter reading the slit-woven texts like runes. There I learned that Daylight Savings Time began as a candle-saving joke by Benjamin Franklin; that the length of a day for a dinosaur was twenty-three hours; that theme parks overestimated wait times for rides, because afterward people reported overestimation as pleasurable and underestimation as agitating; that the Roman calendar originally included sixty-one month-less days of winter; that according to the math of three Spanish scientists, time would eventually stop and ". . . everything will be frozen, like a snapshot of one instant, forever" and that, according to Einstein, the closer you are to the center of the Earth, the slower time passes. It was true then, time passed faster for my head than my heart. Perhaps this was why I still felt my children needed me, though I knew they did not.

In the next exhibit, everyone was lying down, and I was glad for the opportunity, if briefly, to equalize the head/heart time gap. The gallery was dimly lit and furnished with rows of velvet upholstered daybeds of various colors. I snuck a caramel into my mouth from the half-finished package I discovered in my pocket as I stretched out on a red bed near the center. Etched into the ceiling was a backlit portrait of a not unjolly man in skullcap and ruff collar. A recording, activated by my head hitting the pillow, informed me in a breathy whisper that I was gazing into the face of James Ussher, seventeenth century Archbishop of Armagh, who had calculated biblical family histories and concluded that the Earth was created on Saturday, October 22, 4004 BC at 6 p.m.

The specificity of James's finding was interesting, but the featuring of the old miscalculator was puzzling, and I found myself wondering if the archbishop had been a relative of one of the museum's employees. Dear old uncle Jimmy, I thought with a chuckle, picturing the museum's aged doorman in knickers learning cribbage from the Late Archbishop of Armagh. Which made me think of the term "late" for deceased and how it was built into the language to hold it against the dead for never being on time. Which reminded me of my late husband who, in the days of his life had been pathologically prompt. Had his precision, I wondered now, been an unconscious attempt to undo the effects of his impending perpetual lateness? And how many of what we experience as irritations are in fact, unreceived gifts?

I slipped another caramel in my mouth and let the candy rest on my tongue, the sweet saliva stew pooling until another guard tapped me on the shoulder and asked me to move on.

Soon I came upon a large vending machine, next to which was a shelf piled with tokens. I followed the visitor in front of me and did as she did—that is, I took a token from the shelf, inserted it into the vending machine, and pressed the gold button. Out dropped a booklet. I was instructed to take my booklet and step into the reading area, which was a circle of leather beanbag chairs. As

I maneuvered onto a free beanbag, my knees touched the leg of the man sitting next to me, and for a fraught moment, we seemed to recognize one another, though the recognition quickly turned cold, leaving in its place an awkward shiver of sympathy.

My booklet contained a story about a fisherwoman translated from an unspecified ancient language. In the story, the fisherwoman came upon a group of children torturing a small starfish. She took pity on the starfish and placed it back into the sea. The next day the fisherwoman was visited by a huge starfish who told her the small starfish she'd saved was the Prince of the Sea, and the Queen of the Sea wanted to thank her personally. So, the fisherwoman traveled to the Palace under the Sea where she met the prince and stayed for three days, after which she asked to return to her husband. The prince gave her a magic box to keep her safe and told her never to open it. When the fisherwoman arrived in her village, three hundred years had passed. Nothing was recognizable. Grief-stricken, the fisherwoman opened the box, at which point she fell to the ground a weak, old woman. I found the story deeply disturbing.

The Time Museum was said to be the museum that elicited the widest range of emotions of any of the world's museums. And indeed, on one end of the restroom corridor was the Crying Room and on the other end was the Laughing Room. Whether the rooms were meant as shared gathering spaces or containers for the relief of emotional urges, they were both surprisingly contagious, such that a trip to the restroom, depending upon which direction one entered and exited the corridor, risked one's equanimity to such an extreme that visitors often avoided the toilet entirely and sometimes to their great embarrassment (hence the robust inventory of Time Museum sweatpants on sale at the gift shop and the many visitors I saw walking around in them, the most popular of which was the gray sweatpants with white lettering across the rear that read: WHAT YOU SEE IS ALREADY IN THE PAST). I had to pee but decided to hold it.

Just then, a gloved museum employee in coat and tails emerged to announce a special panel discussion on the topic, "What time is it really?" about to get underway. We were ushered forward to an auditorium with swivel chairs placed around a rotating stage upon which sat the speakers—a panel of experts in various fields from astronomy to philosophy to religion to physics. Discussion was made of the hyperplane of space and rotations of the time axis, and after God knew how long, I slunk off, stupefied and headached. The lecture, which seemed not to have an end, had made me ravenous.

The way to the café was marked by an enormous timeline silkscreened on tall, foldable panels. From the Big Bang, it took me sixty steps to reach the extinction of the dinosaurs, then just one more to reach the appearance of modern humans and a toe tip more to the invention of the veggie burger. Which was the only food served in the café, though it came with a choice of potato or kale crisps, and an orange. Musicians playing thumb harps wove their way around the tables adding a ceremonious twang to the meal.

Once my appetite was sated, I ducked into the restroom, past the Laughing Room, and my resultant giggling eased the passing of liquid even after the long wait. As I left the stall, I noticed a number of women staring into the mirror that hung above the bank of sinks. I slipped between two, put my hands under the faucet, looked up at my reflection, and my eyes met a younger version of myself in a tunic with shoulder pads. It was the outfit I'd worn when I'd first met my husband. My cheeks were rounder than I was used to, and dark blue eyeshadow glittered on my lids. I was quite beautiful. A label underneath the mirror stated: THIS IS THE AGE YOU FEEL. The woman next to me gasped, and I peeked at her reflection: a stooped and balding crone in a burlap sack. When I looked at her directly, I saw she was, in fact, stylishly dressed and not a day over forty. On the way out was another mirror, this one full-length. All distortion and strangeness—there I stood naked with a child's round belly but saggy, liver-spotted knees. My breasts hung low and deflated, while my shoulders and nose peeled with the sunburns of pre-melanoma days. I did not care to linger over the label. Perhaps it said, "This is the age your body parts feel." I quickly exited the restroom, hands over my ears. Tears filled my eyes as I passed the Crying Room.

In short order I arrived at the edge of a time pool in
which several visitors were treading water, while others
breaststroked against the surface which met them like a
lap machine, such that they paddled madly but made little
progress. Still others were on their backs floating slowly
backward. I walked the perimeter of the pool, gazing at
water which remained impressively clear but shifted in
color from turquoise to jade to gold as my vantage changed.
The breaststrokers were panting audibly; the floaters kept
periodically lifting their heads to orient themselves, the
treaders were tense with concentration, reminding me
of amateur meditators. Each group regarded the other
with a condescension I found unbecoming, and which I
thought betrayed a secret envy. Had I fancied getting wet,
surely, I would have sidestroked through the treaders neither battling nor surrendering to the pool's current.

Next, I found myself amid a display of wooden lecterns,
each housing a screen, a toggle switch, and a silver knob.
As I stepped forward to one of the free lecterns, its screen
began playing scenes of my life. There I was, sitting on my
old couch, watching *The Sopranos,* and nursing my newborn son. I turned the silver knob to the left and watched
as my son's cheek dimpled then fattened with each suck-
ling draw, and my early-mother eyes blinked so slowly it
seemed I was falling asleep between each of his gulps. I
flipped the toggle, and I was lying in a hospital bed with an
IV dripping steroids into my arm as my mother knitted by
my side. I turned the knob to the right, and the IV emptied

into me and the nurse ran in with a benzo which I gulped down with water and from my mother's clicking needles flew a scarf, a hat and mittens to match. This was power. To control which moments to slow and which to speed. I accelerated right through my school days—the stomach flus, the periods, the lemon juice hair bleaches, the binging and purging, the sound and light shows, the mosh pit, the bad trip, the first dates, the date rape, the accident, the breakup.

Then I decelerated one Sunday morning a year and half ago when I'd sat at the kitchen table cupping my mug of coffee as its warmth spread into my palms, and the caffeine draped its blanket of contentment over me, and I turned from the view out the window of the mountain that did not move to the doorway, through which walked my husband, whom I hadn't seen since I slipped from our bed, and who was heading toward me now, arms open, intoning my full name as if it were a precious stone he'd dropped long ago and just now found and was holding to the light exclaiming how beautifully it glowed.

There was, I noticed, no pause button on the lectern. This struck me as both painful and useful. I could slow my son bending down to kiss me before disappearing into the train that would take him to his home that was no longer our home, but I could not stop him. I could slow the song my daughter sang in the shower and listen as her singing poured through the cracked open door on a plume of steam festooning the house in strawberries and silk, but I could not prevent her from turning off the shower and stepping out. "Can you feel it?" she used to say, I now remembered. "The quickening?" as she'd wave her little hands in the air to indicate time's gust. I sneezed, and as soon as my hands left the lectern, the screen went blank.

At the Sumerian water clock, there was a commotion. The guards were trying to get visitors to move on, but they were refusing to leave. I pushed my way closer and saw the large stone bowl originally filled with water that was slowly draining through the spout at the bottom. Inside the bowl, hours were marked based on the water level, but I quickly ascertained that the water, having reached a certain lower level, was barely trickling out. In contrast to time's ticking faster as they aged, visitors to the Sumerian water clock witnessed time slowing as the day wore on, and no one wanted to go. People were skipping and dancing, in celebration of time given back. To me, however, the scene felt melancholy. As if they were wooing an illusion.

I continued to the gift shop.

It was hard to decide what to get amid the sundials and the pendulums and the sand sculptures. I wandered the rows of celestial charts, chronometers, chronologies, and cosmologies. I fingered a purple Chronos statuette, a leather-bound copy of the Zohar, and flipped through texts by Descartes, Kant, Heidegger, Hawking, and Zeno. There was a lovely hologram of Einstein I briefly considered and some light cones that I thought might look nice on a coffee table placed over one of the Big Bang rugs. I passed on the plush arrow of time and the medicine box of stimulants and depressants, though they were each tempting. The pocket-sized DeLorean and glittery weekly planners were overpriced. In the end, I purchased a tight-fitting T-shirt with lettering across the chest that read, ALL DIMENSIONS ARE SUBJECT TO CHANGE.

As I headed toward the exit, a young girl wearing a museum badge that said LITTLE DISCLAIMER stepped in front of me and said, "Nothing you have experienced today proves in any way that there is such a thing, in fact, as time. Thank you for visiting."

I didn't quite wish to leave just yet, so I stood by the door, eavesdropping on the other visitors as they left. Those who'd arrived at the Time Museum looking for action found nothing much happened. Those who came for personal development, instead of epiphanies found only echoes and doubles of themselves. Some people felt it was all a sham, others felt it was the best spent time of their lives. "Time has changed everything for me," I heard one man say.

Finally, I made my way out the door, along the path, and through the arch of the exit gate, where I paused to look out at the city below. Time's shadow spilled over me onto the road ahead, and then dark clouds began to gather. I started down the road that wound to the cable car station and soon was drenched. Looking for a straighter route, I ran down the hill over a fuchsia carpet of creeping thyme. In my mind's eye, my children rolled down the spread of blooms, and my husband held an umbrella over my head. Little raindrop-sized holes opened everywhere.

ACKNOWLEDGMENTS

MY HEARTFELT THANKS TO so many people who have helped me in my fiction writing journey. To Matt Bell, for selecting this collection for publication, whose endorsement of these stories rallied me at just the right time. To Christine Stroud and everyone at Autumn House who worked tirelessly so this book could put its best foot forward when stepping into the world. To Kinsley Stocum for the gorgeous cover design. To my incomparable writers' group—Felicia Berliner, Pamela Erens, Joanne Serling, Therese Eiben, and Philip Moustakis, who supported, challenged, and cheered these stories through all of their growing pains. To Gillian Cummings for reading an early draft of the collection and helping to choose which stories made the cut. To Steve Yarbrough and Bobbie Ann Mason for genuine encouragement and buoying support. To Emily Nemens for sharp editorial vision and ongoing championing. To Sabrina Orah Mark for modeling inventiveness and sharing her excitement. To Jonathan Lethem for honoring one of these stories as the winner of *BOMB*'s fiction contest. To Laura Marie for enthusiasm and advocacy. To the Vermont Studio Center and Sewanee Writers' Conference for providing space and inspiration and introducing me to so many wonderful artists and writers. To my parents for fostering in me the love of creating. And deepest gratitude as always to Gregg, Jonah, and Eva whose love reminds me on a daily basis of what's most important.

NEW AND FORTHCOMING
FROM AUTUMN HOUSE PRESS

Murmur by Cameron Barnett

2023 DONALD JUSTICE POETRY PRIZE, SELECTED BY MARK JARMAN
Ghost Man on Second by Erica Reid

2023 RISING WRITER PRIZE IN FICTION, SELECTED BY MATT BELL
Half-Lives by Lynn Schmeidler

Nest of Matches by Amie Whittemore

2023 AUTUMN HOUSE POETRY PRIZE, SELECTED BY JANUARY GILL O'NEIL
Book of Kin by Darius Atefat-Peckham

2023 AUTUMN HOUSE FICTION PRIZE, SELECTED BY PAM HOUSTON
Near Strangers by Marian Crotty

2023 AUTUMN HOUSE NONFICTION PRIZE, SELECTED BY JENNY BOULLY
Deep & Wild Places: A Life in West Virginia by Laura Jackson

2023 CAAPP BOOK PRIZE, SELECTED BY NICOLE SEALEY
Terminal Maladies by Okwudili Nebeolisa

For our full catalog please visit autumnhouse.org.